"You boys come in here looking for me?"

Raider figured they were both in their early twenties, almost kids, that they were fast, but that was all. . . . Young, mean, fast—that could be a deadly combination. It usually was.

"You better put your shooting irons on the bar in front of you," he said. "The barkeep will hold them for you till you leave."

Gamblers were scooping their money off the tables and moving fast, and things had gone very quiet. There was no way the two gunnies could go on ignoring Raider and keep their pride intact. The way he was playing it there wasn't any out, there could only be winner and loser, no matter how things were settled.

It was plain which Raider expected to be. . . .

J.D. HARDIN

HELL ON THE
POWDER RIVER

BERKLEY BOOKS, NEW YORK

HELL ON THE POWDER RIVER

A Berkley Book/published by arrangement with
the author

PRINTING HISTORY
Berkley edition/June 1987

ISBN: 0-425-09895-8

PRINTED IN THE UNITED STATES OF AMERICA

CHAPTER ONE

"Throw down the box!" yelled the man who stepped suddenly from behind a rock as the stagecoach labored at a snail's pace up a sharp incline.

The driver and guard were taken by surprise and found themselves looking down into the unforgiving twin eyes of a double-barrel shotgun.

"Hold up on them horses or I'll blast you both off that bench, so there won't be nothing but bones and boot leather left of either of you," the bandit yelled from beneath the flour sack that covered his head and shoulders. His eyes, glittering in two circular holes cut in the sack, looked strangely like those of a snake.

The driver pulled hard on the lines and brought the three pairs of sweating horses to a halt on the rutted stony hillside. He engaged the brake blocks to prevent the coach from rolling backward downhill. The guard's right hand lay on the stock of the shotgun on the seat beside him, but he made no move to lift this weapon or go for his revolver. Both he and the driver were well aware of the six rifle barrels pointing at them from behind rocks beyond the screening manzanita brush.

The bandit repositioned himself after the horses stopped so he was not vulnerable to a shot from inside

1

the coach through one of the side windows. If any of the passengers wanted to shoot him, they would have to extend a head and an arm outside the coach. At this close range of ten feet or so, the barrel of buckshot would certainly separate the arm from its owner, if not the head also, and the bandit would still have the second barrel for the guard and driver.

"Throw down the box!" the holdup man shouted again.

The guard tossed down the locked metal strongbox, and it hit the dirt close to the bandit's feet.

"You two fellas lay down your guns on the bench," the robber ordered, "and get yourselves down here right quickly." He called back over his shoulder, "Either of these varmints make one false move, boys, you plug 'em good."

With the shotgun and six rifle barrels trained on them, the driver and guard felt they had no option but to obey. The driver was ordered to unhitch the six horses, while the guard placed stones behind the coach wheels to help the brakes hold it on the slope.

"You passengers stay put and no harm will come to you," the bandit called so they could hear him inside the coach.

Of the seven passengers, two held pocket revolvers at the ready. Both looked like businessmen, and they clutched their weapons nervously and inexpertly, clearly having no wish for gunplay. The two women in the coach sat pale, still, and frightened, waiting for the worst to happen. They were thin and severe-looking, like schoolmarms or missionary ladies, but no strangers to life out west. Two of the remaining male passengers were unarmed—one was a dull-witted farmboy and the other a pimply underweight clerk. The seventh passenger stank of cheap whiskey and, beneath his black Stetson, seemed only half aware of what was going on, much to the ladies' disgust.

They had been terrified of this big rough-looking man with a six-gun on his hip who had snored loudly and fallen against them in his sleep as the coach jolted over rough ground. Since none of the gentlemen present seemed to have the nerve to point out to this sleeping desperado that he was leaning in an almost indecent posture against one of the ladies, her friend had tapped him smartly on the knee with the handle of her furled parasol. He had opened his eyes, smiled, and winked at her. This caused the lady to flush, because there was no denying that in spite of his rough appearance the man was very handsome. Both ladies had noticed his jet black eyes, long black mustaches, and the six-foot-two-inch muscular body beneath the flannel shirt, battered leather jacket, and sun-bleached jeans.

"Do you think there's any danger of . . . ?" She did not have to finish her question for the other woman to know what she was talking about, which happened to be their possible rape by the bandits.

"They're all animals," she said.

"Do you think that maybe if we threw our purses out, he might spare us?"

"It's a faint hope, but it's worth a try."

The bandit had directed the guard and driver to walk the team of six horses some distance away, and he was prying the lid off the metal strongbox with a small crowbar when the two purses came sailing out the coach window. He put down the crowbar and first picked up his shotgun and then the two purses. He approached the coach, bowed, and tossed the purses back inside.

"Like I said, I wasn't planning no harm against any

of you. I don't want your money—only what's in the box. You sit back quiet now and let me get on with my work."

He backed away slowly, gun at the ready, until he was out of direct view of the coach windows. Then he put down his shotgun and went about breaking the strongbox lock again.

In possession of their purses once more, the two women looked somehow disappointed that nothing more dramatic had happened. The one with the parasol rapped the knee of the big man in the leather jacket, and he gave her the kind of look he might give a mosquito, which made her plenty mad.

"Why don't you do something?" she asked in a loud stage whisper.

"It ain't in my nature," he told her with a lazy grin.

Properly fuming now, she said to him, "You flop down here in a whiskey haze and we all worry in case you might be about to start some trouble with innocent people. You look just the kind to do it. But when something happens when you could be of some use, you just rest yourself and don't do a thing."

Her friend goaded her on. "I think he may be in cahoots with the robbers. Better be careful what you say."

"I don't care, they can shoot me if they wish," she declared. "I won't be told what to say. Is it true?" she rapped the man on the knee with her parasol handle again. "Are you in league with these unprincipled wretches?"

"No, ma'am," the man said.

"Is that all you have to say for yourself?" she demanded to know.

"Yes, ma'am."

Frustrated by his uncaring, lackadaisical attitude and

the silent passivity of the other men, she leaned out the window to see what was going on. The driver and guard were almost a mile down the trail with the horses. The bandit had succeeded in opening the strongbox, and he was now holding in one hand two large clinking bags which she guessed were filled with gold coins. With the other hand he was stuffing greenbacks taken from ripped-open express packages into various pockets, not bothering to pick up those that fell to the ground.

She pulled her head back in before he spotted her and told the other passengers in an urgent voice, "He's ready to make his getaway. Someone, do something."

When no one did anything, she reached across to grab the pocket revolver of the man sitting opposite her. She would probably have snatched it from his hand had not the man in the leather jacket brushed her arm away at the last moment.

"You got spirit, lady, and I have to admire that," he said to her pleasantly. "But that bandit has a scattergun, and buckshot ain't good for the complexion."

That quieted both the women for a while, and none of the male passengers showed any interest in fight. After a minute, they heard footsteps and the clinking of coin bags outside the coach.

"You people stay put and you won't die or get robbed," the bandit shouted in at them. "Your driver and guard will bring back the horses after me and my men leave. You won't be no worse off than maybe an hour late on your journey. But you try leaving this coach and we'll pick you off, sure as there's a sun in the sky."

The passengers listened in silence to the bandit's footsteps as he walked away. They were surprised when the man in the leather jacket got to his feet and reached in the luggage rack over their heads for his carbine.

"I told you he was in cahoots with them," one woman hissed to the other.

The big man ignored her, quietly opened the coach door, and stepped down. The metallic scrape of a cartridge being levered into the chamber of the Model 94 Winchester .30-30 carbine caused the bandit to wheel around. He dropped the two coin bags and aimed with the shotgun.

"There's almost forty yards between us," the passenger with the carbine told him. "Your scattergun ain't going to have much effect at that range, while this here little carbine is just raring to show its stuff. I suggest you hold your fire, mister, unless you want a taste of lead."

The bandit lowered the shotgun barrels. "I just have to give the signal and six riflemen will open fire on you. Look around."

The big man smiled. "I looked around where the stagecoaches were held up back at Robertson and Lone-tree. Both times they had a bunch of riflemen covering one lone holdup man, like your setup here. But when I looked around where the rifles were, all I saw was one set of bootprints in the dirt."

"You're taking an awful chance, mister," the bandit told him.

"I don't believe there's anybody up there behind them rifles or I'd have heard from them by now. My name's Raider, and I'm a Pinkerton. I been looking for you and kinda figured you were heading out this way. I suppose if I hadn't been so unkind to interrupt, you'd have gathered up them long guns and ridden off. You can lay down that scattergun and take that sack off your head, 'cause I'm taking you in."

Seeing that his bluff with the rifles had failed this

time, and knowing a shotgun was useless against a carbine at forty yards, the bandit threw down the weapon beside the coin bags. But he didn't remove the sack from over his head and shoulders, which Raider took as an indication that he might not have completely given up yet, although he wasn't wearing a six-gun on his hip.

"I been on your trail nearly five weeks," the Pinkerton told him. "You ain't shot anyone that I know of, so no one is going to string you up."

"Hell, eight or ten years in a penitentiary is worse than any lynching."

"You know what they say," Raider told him. "If you can't serve the time, don't do the crime." He pointed. "Stand in the shade of that rock and empty your pockets. When the driver and guard get back, we'll truss you up and take you and your horse along with us. Where's it hitched?"

"Other side of this hill."

The outlaw obeyed him meekly enough. He walked to the shade and began producing from his pockets the greenbacks he had taken from the express packages. Raider picked up the shotgun and eased both cocked hammers gently onto the firing pins. He put the shotgun and his own carbine under his left arm and clutched the two coin bags by their necks in his left hand. As he walked back toward the coach, whose occupants had still not emerged, his right hand hung free. A lot of wise folks would have seen this as a message. Not the holdup man. He thought this was a good time to go for his concealed gun. Instead of greenbacks, from one pocket he pulled a Smith & Wesson .32 and tried a fast shot at the Pinkerton.

Raider was big, which made him an easier target than most men. This was a major part of the reason he relied on his fast draw and intended to quit the Pinkertons as soon as he noticed himself slowing by so much as a whisker of time. He needed to be fast enough to stop the other man from getting off his first shot. He had been expecting this outlaw to pull something, and chances were it would be a concealed gun. This was no surprise. It would be no sweat. Raider even waited that extra fraction of a second to let the bandit think he had the drop on him.

Then, fast as a sidewinder's strike, the Pinkerton's right palm hit the wood grips of his Remington .44 revolver. Cumbersome in the hands of most men, the heavy long-barrel six-shooter, at Raider's touch, seemed to leap from its holster with a life of its own. He snapped back the hammer with his right thumb as he leveled the barrel at his opponent's midgut, and then he squeezed the trigger.

The cartridge exploded, and the big .44 spat flame. The bandit took the slug in his lower chest an instant before his forefinger was set to tighten on the trigger of his .32. He never got to fire the shot. Instead of his trigger finger tightening, his knees buckled and he slumped on the stony ground. The Pinkerton watched his body fall. The light had already gone out of the outlaw's eyes, and a trickle of blood ran from the corner of his mouth when the sack was pulled off.

The woman with the furled parasol waved it at Raider from the stagecoach window and shouted, "It took you long enough to sober up and stick it to that no-good bum. I was wondering when you'd get around to it. I knew from the moment I set eyes on you that you were a murderous son of a bitch."

• • •

The five horsemen drove the sheep in front of them. The huge flock of more than a thousand sheep moved as a single white woolly mass over the land as the frightened animals, packed close together, ran first one way and then another. The horsemen drove them harder, firing occasional shots from their six-guns to panic the sheep further. Their tiny hooves drummed on the hard ground in short rapid steps, causing the earth to vibrate beneath them. A herd of longhorns could do the same when they had a mind to run, but it was not so remarkable with big heavy animals like cattle or, heavier still, buffalo. These sheep might be nothing much when taken singly, but this running flock was an enormous tide of bobbing white bodies, making a hell of a racket with their *baa*ing and raising a high column of dust behind them.

The five riders were brutal to the sheep near them, knocking and trampling them with their horses, shooting them with their revolvers. One man lashed them with a stock whip, downing those animals he hit directly on the head. The men yelled and cursed. The sheep grew more fearful, packed tighter together, and ran faster, the flock streaming off in new directions like quicksilver. But the riders galloped up along the sides, and the lead sheep veered to avoid them, moving straight ahead again.

Flock and riders passed over a rise. Ahead a wagon was stopped in the deep grass, and an unharnessed mule grazed nearby, which looked up in alarm at the approaching flock of sheep. The panic-stricken animals kept charging straight ahead, and some of them no doubt would have been pushed into the wagon, destroying it and killing themselves, had not a man suddenly risen from the grass near the wagon and frightened the sheep into a new direction.

The sheep surged onward, and the man stood where he was and looked at them as they charged over the edge of a high bluff, unable to stop because of the pressure from those behind, which had not yet seen this sudden drop. The riders hollered like demons and shot their guns in the air to keep the flock moving at full speed. Some of the sheep broke away at the sides, but the majority went over the edge and plunged to death on the rocks below. The five men rode to the cliff edge and looked down at the piles of woolly bodies. Then they pulled their bandannas over their noses to cover their faces and headed toward the man standing by the wagon.

The wagon was loaded with crates, many of which contained medicine bottles. Canvas banners on the wagon sides read: DOCTOR WEATHERBEE—HOMEO-PATHIC MEDICINES—FREE CONSULTATION.

"I guess we owe you our thanks, Doc, for helping us guide them damn nuisance sheep where they belong," one of the riders said to the standing man.

Doc Weatherbee was dressed in the latest back-east big-city style, with a gray worsted wool suit, an indigo blue silk vest, a silk shirt, and a pearl gray derby. Out here in the middle of nowhere, the dust settling down about, he looked like he had just stepped out of a fashionable tailor's store.

Doc Weatherbee said to the man, "I was protecting my wagon, not helping you kill some other man's sheep."

"You a sheep lover, Doc?" one of the riders jeered.

"Take it easy," another cautioned. "I can see why a man might be upset at what he's seen, 'specially if he's a city man and can't hardly tell a cow from a sheep in the first place. Some dudes I've met hardly knew which end the grass went in and which end it came out. But I ain't blaming you for that, Doc, or saying you're ignorant, considering you're a medical man. What you don't know, I bet, is that us cattlemen are fighting for our lives against them sheepherders. Cows eat grass and it grows again, but sheep eat the bunch grass down to its roots and kill it. Once a flock of sheep crosses a range, it's finished for cattle. We got only one solution, us cattlemen, and that's to organize. What you seen in action today is the Oneida County Sheep Shooters Association, the finest group of its kind in all Idaho, even if I do say so myself. Course we can't always shoot all the critters. When there's too many of them, like you saw today, we have to run 'em over a cliff."

"Our rifle barrels would be melted by now if we had tried to shoot them all," another explained.

"Maybe you could sell us something to put in the well water, Doc, which wouldn't harm cattle but would kill off them woolly pests. We'd pay you real good for it."

Weatherbee looked at this man for a moment before he said, "You going to have to pay me all right, Mr. Porter."

"What did you call me?" the man snapped. "My name ain't Porter."

"Yes it is," Doc said. "And that's Mr. O'Neill and Mr. Thompson. I'm sure I could find the names of the remaining two gentlemen without much trouble when I go back to Stone."

"Don't be too sure you're ever going to see that town again," one man said menacingly.

"Hear me out," Weatherbee responded. "I've been to

your ranches peddling my medicines, and I gave you value for your money. Yet, truth to tell, I'm a Pinkerton operative here to collect three thousand in gold coins for the sheep the Oneida County Sheep Shooters Association destroyed two months ago over by Samaria." Doc pulled out his Pinkerton identification papers and held them up for inspection.

"What if we was to tell you we don't know nothing about them sheep killings over by Samaria?" Porter asked.

"I'd say you were liars," Doc told him.

"That's a mighty dangerous thing for a lone man not carrying a gun, so far as I can see, to call five armed men."

"You thinking of running me over the edge too?" Weatherbee asked with a cool smile. "Well, forget it. It's not exactly the best-kept secret in Oneida County who the members of your association are. You're going to be in heavy trouble enough about all these dead sheep, but if they find a dead Pinkerton along with them, you'll be bringing down more trouble on your heads than you know how to handle."

Weatherbee let this sink in. When none of them responded, he went on, "Now, I'm not a law-enforcement officer in the general sense. I'll certainly report this incident to our Chicago office. But I'm not duty-bound to drive my wagon into the town of Stone and report as an eyewitness prepared to testify. I'd certainly be tempted to do just that when I arrive. All the same, if I were to be paid that three thousand in gold coins, I could be persuaded to head south to Utah and give Stone a complete miss. I'd have to make that decision before sundown."

They bitched and argued for a while before they rode a ways apart to talk among themselves out of Weatherbee's earshot. Doc knew they were coming to a cold-blooded decision on whether to pay up or kill him. The three he recognized were all big landowners, and Doc figured they stood to lose too much by killing a Pinkerton. That was much the same as poking a hornet's nest. Chicago would flood the area with operatives and keep them in place until they got results. Even out here in Oneida County, folks were aware of the Pinkerton reputation.

Porter rode back to him alone. "You'll get the money. We'll bring it to you first thing tomorrow morning. You be in Snowville, south of the Utah border."

Doc nodded and watched them ride away. He waited until they were out of sight beyond the rise before he called, "You can come out now."

A beautiful woman, stark naked, rose out of the high grass thirty yards away. "I was sure those sheep were going to kill me. I felt sorry for them. Then I was certain my uncle would see me hiding in the grass."

Doc laughed. "I guess if Porter had seen his niece naked with me, it might have weakened my case."

She pulled off his cravat and unbuttoned his vest. "You sure got dressed fast when you heard those sheep coming. That's one thing against putting all your clothes in a wagon so insects can't crawl into them. I didn't even have a leaf big enough to cover me, unless I was to make a grass skirt, and I had no time for that." She had him stripped to the waist by now. "I come out all this way for a little peace and privacy, and what happens? A lousy relative tries to run me over with sheep. He's got the whole of Idaho and most of Utah to chase them over, but he has to head them toward me while I'm nude in the grass with a snake-oil salesman. How come you never told me you were a Pinkerton?"

"In case you'd warn your uncle."

"Fair enough," she said, and smiled. "I would have, too."

"I know."

He kicked off his boots and stepped out of his pants. He was pleased that the mass killing of the sheep had not interfered with her emotional and physical desires. A girl back east would have had the vapors for days after witnessing such a thing—but this was a western gal who knew better than to allow such happenings to interfere with her pleasures.

She made Doc chase her over the grassland, and when he caught her, she carefully chose a patch of thick soft grass on which to fall. He lay beside her and feasted his eyes and hands on her lush body. Her rosebud nipples jutted from white supple flesh. Her skin felt silky smooth under his hands as he stroked her gently. As his erection rose, the tip of his cock touched her thigh and she lowered one hand to caress his engorged organ.

CHAPTER TWO

Cole Brent stepped off the eastbound train in Chicago. He waved away a porter and carried his grip himself. He scowled at no one in particular, hoping this would make him look older than his sixteen years, hoping also it would hide the fear he was feeling at being alone in this noisy, fast-moving city. He had thought Cheyenne and Omaha big on the journey east, but they were nothing to Chicago. Back home in Oregon, he could have imagined places like Cheyenne and Omaha. Chicago was something a human being had to see to believe. And he reckoned he had only seen a piece of it from the railroad car windows as his train came in.

He had to wait a long time on the curb before he risked crossing the street, which had all kinds of wagons, traps, and conveyances moving at great speed in two directions. Cole would not think twice about riding in among a herd of half-wild longhorns to rope a calf for branding, but he could get no grip on all this speeding city traffic with the wheels and horses' hooves clattering on the cobblestones. Taking his opportunity, he dashed wildly across the street to a cab rank. He gave the driver the address on Fifth Avenue and climbed inside with his bag. The driver flicked his whip, and the pair of black horses pulled the cab into the stream of vehicles. There was no sign of a cow or a sheep, men didn't walk around with rifles, the women dressed like he'd seen in newspaper pictures, there probably weren't even any rattlers or gophers, let alone bears, and a helluva lot of the men looked sober and clean-shaven. Chicago was a mighty strange place.

The buildings all had numbers here; 191–193 Fifth Avenue was a dignified stone building. He gave the cab driver a silver dollar and climbed the steps to the door. A man dressed in black like an undertaker met him inside and asked what he wanted. He was polite, yet Cole noticed his hard eyes and powerful hands.

"I've come to see Mr. Pinkerton," he said.

"Which Mr. Pinkerton? There's three of them."

"Three?"

"Father and sons. You ain't going to see none of them without having an appointment, young fella."

Cole was intimidated. All the same, the reference to him as "young fella" stung him, and he determined to brazen it out. "I've come to see the Pinkerton who put this outfit together."

"That would be Mr. Allan Pinkerton. Who wants to see him?"

"Cole Brent."

The man looked down his nose at him. "That you?"

"Yes."

"Mr. Pinkerton's busy."

"Tell him I'm Blind Danny's son."

The man pointed to a chair and left Cole in the hallway. After a few minutes he reappeared and beckoned. Cole picked up his grip and followed. He was shown into a high-ceilinged, somber office. A big, powerful-looking man sat behind a huge polished desk. He eyed Cole in a not overfriendly way. The man who had shown him in stayed directly behind him.

"Blind Danny's son, eh?" he asked in a strong Scots accent.

"Yes, sir."

"I don't know any Blind Danny," Allan Pinkerton said, asking before the youth could reply, "Can you use a revolver?"

"Yes, sir."

"I thought so. Next you'll be telling me you're twenty-one years old. Have you any idea how many boys your age run away from home and bang on our door to say they've come to be Pinkerton operatives?"

"No, sir."

"Neither do I, because I don't count them. I tell them all what I'm going to tell you. Come back in five years."

"But I don't want to be a Pinkerton operative, sir."

"You don't?" Allan Pinkerton looked surprised and angry. "What is it then, you wee twerp? Are we not good enough for you?"

"That's not what I meant. My father thinks the world of you, sir. That's why he sent me here."

"Blind Danny?"

"He wants a couple of your best operatives, Mr. Pinkerton. He said that if you were not inclined to believe me, I should show you this."

Cole stepped forward and placed his grip on the polished desk. He opened it and rooted around inside. First he pulled out a pair of thick wool socks and placed them on the desk. Then a Colt Peacemaker; the .45 was worn and scratched from use, which caused Pinkerton and the man behind Cole to exchange a look. Next he produced a red flannel shirt. Then finally a buckskin bag. He untied the rawhide thong threaded through the bag's neck and emptied the bag's contents out on the desk to form a gleaming pile of twenty-dollar gold pieces.

"He said to show you this," Cole repeated.

Pinkerton smiled. "Blind Danny sounds like a wise man. Tell me, wasn't he worried about you carrying this amount?"

Cole patted the Colt on the desk. "He figured I can handle anybody east of Nebraska. I'm fairly quick with a gun. He told me not to play cards with anyone on the train."

"From where?"

"Kelton, Utah."

"You from thereabouts?"

"No, up in Baker City, Oregon. But we don't have no railroads or practically nothing up there. My father being blind and all, and not wanting anyone to know he was sending for help, decided he couldn't come here himself. So he sent me, saying I was going to school for a year in the East. If they thought he was sending for outside help, they'd shoot him right away. My father says the only reason we're both still alive is because I'm too young to be a threat and he's blind."

"Sit down, young man, and we'll both have a cup of tea," the big Scotsman said kindly. "Then you'd better tell me your story from the beginning."

Evanston was a railroad town on the Southern Pacific, in the southwestern corner of Wyoming, not many miles west from where the Union Pacific met the Southern Pacific at Granger. The town was close to the Utah border and had its share of Mormons, only they had little say in the running of the place. Most people seemed to be just passing through, and the residents sold them things they might need, everything from horseshoes to whiskey. Raider stayed in a rooming house, hit the bars, lost some money at cards and some more on a red-haired woman who hailed from Tennessee. He had sent his telegram to the Chicago office announcing that his mission had been accomplished. He was now free until he got his next assignment, which would come by telegram also. He whooped it up while he could, knowing that Allan Pinkerton hated to have an idle man on his payroll. The Chicago office would find something for him to do soon enough. A lot of men might have been upset to be stuck in a backward jerkwater town like Evanston. Not Raider. This was his kind of place, where there were no pillars of society telling him he must improve himself and not much in the way of rules and regulations.

He walked over to the Western Union office every afternoon, and soon enough a telegram was there for him. He opened the yellow sheet and read the clerk's neat copperplate writing.

Your report on the case just completed is totally inadequate. Times, locations, circumstances must be supplied. At your earliest convenience, send a revised report supplying a detailed account of the events. Your next assignment is at Baker City, Oregon. Meet client's son, Cole Brent, and Weatherbee at Kelton, Utah, this Thursday.

Wagner

Wagner was his office contact in Chicago, and while he complained of getting no details on Raider's last case, he himself transmitted no details about what Raider could expect in Oregon, which was a form of revenge, Raider supposed. So Weatherbee would be on this case too. At least he wouldn't be hard to find, with his city finery, in a town like Kelton, which Raider guessed was much the same as the town he was in presently. As usual he was of two minds about working a case with Doc. He liked the man for his dependability and courage as a Pinkerton operative, while at the same time Doc drove him crazy with his superior ways, the jokes he played on him, the way he stole women out from under his nose, and lastly his strict obedience to Pinkerton regulations. Raider figured there was give and take with any partner on a case—if only Weatherbee didn't pick on him, just left him be, they would work together fine.

Kelton was only about ten local stops down the Southern Pacific line, probably no more than a watering and fueling stop with a freight depot and a few shacks, hopefully at least one of them a saloon.

Porter had showed up alone with the $3,000 in gold coins to pay for the animals the Oneida County Sheep Shooters Association had destroyed near the town of Samaria. He had threatened Doc Weatherbee with death if he showed his face across the Idaho border again. Doc was too busy counting the money to pay him much attention. He put the cash in a Snowville bank so it could be collected by the sheep owners in due time. Then he drove his wagon south to the nearest stop on the Southern Pacific line, which was Kelton.

Doc Weatherbee had purchased the wagon and mule from a genuine traveling physician. At the time he needed a disguise which would let him go where he chose in order to gather information. Doc had correctly guessed that everybody allowed a doctor to be around, even if he was one with doubtful credentials. Better a bad doctor than none at all. It wasn't long before Doc found himself removing .45 slugs from arms and thighs, dispensing ointment for dandruff, pills for sleeplessness or male vigor, soothing advice and some harmless tonic for the many who only imagined themselves ill. This was the cost attached to the disguise. It sure helped a Pinkerton operative to move around undercover when he presented himself as a doctor, but often all that he gained was patients!

Doc was not a man who did things by halves. He had a lively sense of responsibility—in certain areas at least. He now worried about harming innocent people who came to him for advice. So he learned what he could about medicine from books, and by asking various doctors a lot of questions, usually over a bottle of good bourbon, which seemed to assist the medical memory. He discovered for himself what any cowpoke or miner could have told him—that many sawbones out west knew nothing and caused as much harm as good. The truth was, there wasn't much any doctor, no matter how learned and skilled, could do about a .45 bullet that had been lying inside a man's gut for half a day. He was a goner, and that was that. Same way with a lot of the sicknesses that just came sudden on a man. No one really knew what they were, and they either killed or crippled a man or else he got over them. The most even the best doctor could do was try to relieve any pain. The worst a doctor could do was try to fix what he didn't understand.

Weatherbee solved his problems of posing as a doctor by first dumping all the cures and medicines that could cause anyone harm. Now, even if he did recommend the wrong cure, he wasn't going to hurt the patient. His constant rule was to insist that anyone who seemed gen-

uinely seriously ill should see a physician with a college
diploma. Many tough, mean outlaws who were willing
to face down any bounty hunter or federal marshal
chickened out about seeing a doctor. Some of them
would prefer to die like a dog, slowly under a bush,
than face up to what was bothering them and try to cure
it. Weatherbee had managed to bully or shame a lot of
such men into seeking medical help.

His big medical discovery lay in the fact that there
was nothing wrong with most people that a little listening and sympathy couldn't cure. He doled out sugar
pills and charged a good price for them, since no one
was convinced of a cure unless they had to pay a price
for it. A little conversation and a smile from Doc often
worked wonders for ladies who had been feeling poorly,
and the result was that they told their friends and he
ended up swamped with a town's womenfolk and their
chatter while he was supposed to be working on a Pinkerton case. Yet he often learned things from a talkative
woman that he might never have discovered for himself,
things that put him on an inside track in the case under
investigation.

Another unexpected side issue was the mule that
came with the wagon. When a man bought a mule he
expected a stubborn, contrary animal, but even Doc admitted, in spite of his affection for her, that Judith was
more stubborn and contrary than any other mule created
by God—or as Doc would say, Judith had a stronger
and more determined personality. Weatherbee had long
since given up trying to lay down the law to her. He
even enjoyed her contrary behavior when Raider was
around, because it drove his fellow Pinkerton wild.
Raider had developed a strong aversion to the mule,

egged on by Doc's frequent assertions that of the two of them, Judith was the smarter.

Weatherbee allowed Judith to set her own pace on the trail from Snowville to Kelton. He was in Utah, almost due north of the Great Salt Lake, and what had once been dusty wasteland was now cultivated by thrifty and hardworking Mormon farmers. Large tracts were still desolate, beyond the efforts of even the most determined colonizers with their irrigation channels and ceaseless labor. The Mormons were not friendly to outsiders, charging non-Mormon travelers high prices for anything they needed while passing through Utah.

Doc was not concerned. He had bought a copy of every newspaper he could find in Snowville and now he was relaxing as Judith plodded aimlessly along, stopping whenever her fancy took her. Like nearly everyone who could read in the great isolated spaces of the West, Doc followed with fascination the doings of people back east and in Europe. Like most others, he had a low opinion of these people and their doings. However, that did not stop him from keeping track of them through the newspapers. He had completed a detailed report on the Oneida County Sheep Shooters Association case and put it in the U.S. mail at Snowville. In addition, he had forwarded a telegraphic message on the stagecoach to be transmitted from Kelton to Chicago. By the time he arrived in Kelton, he should have a response from headquarters and possibly a new assignment. This would be just fine with him, because he had no wish to be marooned in a tiny town in the middle of nowhere. Time off in a big town or a city went well with Weatherbee, who enjoyed the distractions of urban life.

In time he made it to Kelton and stopped by the

Western Union office. A telegram was there for him. It revealed no more information than was necessary, saying only that he would meet up with Raider and the client's son in this town before setting out for Baker City, Oregon. He was given no clue as to how to recognize this Cole Brent, but he knew Raider wouldn't be too hard to find—all Doc would have to do was poke his head into the noisiest saloon. After finding himself a hotel room and Judith a stable, Doc walked down Main Street, stopped outside the noisiest saloon, looked in, and saw Raider's black hat and black mustaches clear above the head level of the other men standing along the bar. They nodded warily to each other, and Raider poured him a drink from his bottle.

Doc tasted it and grimaced. "Are you drinking this rotgut because it's cheap or because you've intestinal worms you want to clean out?"

"'Fraid you ain't gonna find things here in Kelton up to your eastern standards, Weatherbee," Raider growled.

"I can still find something that won't peel off the insides of my stomach."

Doc Weatherbee was wrong. The barkeep told him proudly that Kelton saloons sold only Kelton-made whiskey. He also observed that strangers stopped complaining after their third glass of it.

"You see this kid?" Raider wanted to know.

"No. I thought you might have."

"I seen who I think it might be. That kid sitting at the table yonder in the far corner. Yesterday I asked him if he was Cole Brent, and he said no. He had a scared look on his face, so he might have been lying. He's been watching me since. I ain't seen any other young fella in town who wasn't with a bunch. I say we try him again."

Doc nodded. Raider often had a strong effect on people. Mostly he scared them. This was all to the good with a lot of the people they had to deal with as Pinkertons, since they needed scaring. The only drawback was that Raider tended to scare nice honest people even more. Doc would have to step in to calm their fears with his friendly ways and smooth talk.

Doc and Raider walked across the crowded saloon to the almost dark and nearly empty corner, beyond the gaming tables, where the youth sat alone at a table, his back to the wall, his eyes watchful in a pale face.

"Cole Brent—" were the only words Doc got out before he found himself looking into the barrel of a .45 Peacemaker.

"You two scumbags can drift off," the youth grated at him in a voice filled more with fright than menace.

This was no consolation to Weatherbee, who knew that a fearful man was even more likely to pull a trigger than an angry one. "Take it easy," he said. "At least till you find out who we are."

"Like I told your buddy yesterday, I ain't Brent Cole. You fellas are picking on the wrong man." He remained seated, pointing the revolver barrel up at Doc's face.

"We're Pinkertons," Doc explained.

"You ain't nothing but scabby drifters trying to pull some scam on me. Move on or I'll plug you both."

Doc laughed. "If we were out to bother you, kid, my partner would have shot you stone dead already."

This upset the youth, who realized that he hadn't been watching the big man closely enough.

Doc leaned his face closer. "Put your gun away and talk."

The barrel of the Peacemaker wavered a little, but it kept pointing at Doc's nose.

Faster than the kid could react, Doc's right hand swept up from underneath the Colt. His fingers closed around the chambers as the youth squeezed the trigger. Doc's grip prevented the chambers from revolving, so the weapon could not fire. Continuing the upward motion of his hand, he forced the revolver barrel upward and back against the V formed by the thumb and index finger on the handle. This broke the youth's grip on the gun, and Weatherbee took it from him.

"We're Pinkertons," Doc said casually, placing the gun on the table in front of its owner. "Ready to talk?"

"I'm Cole Brent all right," the youth admitted. "I was kinda expecting you Pinkertons to be like you were in Chicago—decent respectable men in proper clothes like a businessman would wear. You two look like the sort the marshal runs out of town on a Saturday night."

Doc, of course, dismissed this description of himself as a piece of rustic ignorance and paid no heed to Raider's laughter.

"My father's name is Daniel Brent. He's still known as Blind Danny from his days on the Oregon goldfields, where he sang ballads and played his guitar for years until he had enough gold laid away to buy the leading hotel in Baker City. It used to be called the Majestic Hotel—that's what the sign outside says—but everyone in town calls it Blind Danny's. My father hails from Kentucky. He wasn't in the War Between the States because he'd lost his sight before that, as a child. The family lost everything in the war, and afterward he came out west along with them. He couldn't do what you might call useful work, so he took to learning all the songs and tunes he could. He could play just about anything anyone wanted. He played for the miners the songs they had known back home and also new ones about big strikes or accidents or fights or whatever that was taking place in the goldfields. When the miners were bust he played for nothing. When they were flush they threw gold at him. He didn't drink, gamble, or whore. He put all that gold in the bank and bought hisself that hotel. He married the prettiest girl in town— and a lot of men got mad about that, because they said he couldn't know the difference so an ugly one would have done him just as well. That's my mother. I'm the oldest boy. I've got a younger brother, and one sister older, one younger. You could say all of us is a happy family."

"I've heard about Baker City being on the old Oregon Trail," Raider said, "but I ain't sure whereabouts it is."

"It's on the Powder River, which flows into the Snake. The town is in the hills up in the northeast corner of Oregon State, with the Idaho Territory on the east and the Washington Territory to the north. Folks say it was the worst hellhole spawned by the Oregon Trail, a town known for its crooked games. Since my father settled there, he's been part of every cleanup campaign, and he claims things have been getting better over the years. Things was going so good, he paid out of his own pocket for a courthouse to be built and he acted as supervisor for the election that made Baker City the county seat."

"But an old dog doesn't learn new tricks," Doc prompted.

"That's right. Baker City was set in its ways, and most of them ways was no good. First thing that was said was the election was rigged. Since my father was supervisor, some said it was he done it. Others just laughed and said if you want to fix an election, have a blind man supervise it. It took a while for my father to see the rightness of that remark. He don't like to admit any shortcoming because he can't see. But by the time he started to admit that he was maybe being hood-winked, men had got killed for talking out against corruption and folks were saying my father had to be involved. The town got took over slowly by these corrupt officials, and it's hard at times to tell who's a wrongdoer. Things have gone real bad now. What my father wants is you Pinkertons to clean up the town, and if you can't do that, at least clear his name."

"Does he hold any official position?" Doc asked.

"He's still a city councilman, but he has no real power or say-so in how things get done. He thinks he has, but they let him talk and then do things behind his back which he gets blamed for. He don't want to give up. I don't know all the details, because for the past year I've been living outside town on a ranch we bought. I been running it—my guess is it's my father's idea to keep me outta trouble. He'll tell you hisself who he thinks is to blame, and he told me to say that if it comes out that some things was his fault, he ain't asking you to keep quiet about it. He wants you to call things as you see them."

They got around to discussing how best to get to Baker City from where they were. Cole told them he had come south by stage, on his way to Chicago, and joined the Southern Pacific railroad at Kelton, which was why the town had been set up as their meeting place. Doc Weatherbee had a handful of timetables and his own ideas about how best to get there.

"What kind of trip did you have on that stagecoach?" Weatherbee asked Cole Brent.

"Rough. The trail from Kelton is northward until you hit the Snake River, and you follow its south bank all the way across the Idaho Territory into Oregon. It's about four hundred and fifty miles from here to Baker City, four or five days and nights by stagecoach. Much as I want to get back home, I gotta admit I ain't looking forward to that journey again."

"I don't blame you," Doc said, leafing through his timetables. "The problem is the railroads haven't come to Oregon yet. All the same, there's a cheaper and easier way for us to get to Baker City. It will take longer, but I think it's worth it. We take the train from here to San Francisco, then a steamer up the coast to the Columbia River, then a boat up the river to the point nearest Pendleton. I reckon Baker City is about a hundred miles from the river on the trail through Pendleton and La Grande. That way, Cole, you'll get to see San Francisco and the Pacific Ocean as well as the Columbia River."

"Sounds great," Cole said enthusiastically.

"I'm going by stagecoach," Raider announced. "I ain't going halfway around the world on account of some goddamn mule."

"I see no reason to subject Judith to any unnecessary overland trek of four hundred and fifty miles," Doc said in an annoyed tone.

"If she dies on the way, you could eat her," Raider suggested.

Doc turned to Cole Brent. "I've pointed out the advantages of the train and ship route. The extra days it will take are worth it both in cost and comfort."

"I guess I should be getting back soon as I can," the youth said hesitantly, obviously not wanting to seem to be taking sides in this difference of opinion between the two Pinkertons. "Reckon I should take the stagecoach because I'm in a hurry, though I sure hate to miss seeing San Francisco and all."

There was a coach leaving at first light the next day, and Doc could catch a train west later in the morning.

It turned out that the stagecoach left Kelton well before first light, and as a result Raider and Cole Brent nearly missed it. Assured that they could catch some breakfast at the first station out, they headed off without even a cup of coffee. A fine cold snow fell as they moved into the hills. The higher they climbed, the larger the flakes got. By the time it was full daylight, they could hardly see through the blizzard, but the driver knew his route and pushed his horses on.

The only other passenger in the coach was a miner, still drunk and now passed out. For once Raider had no hangover. He had béen dog tired and had gone to bed early the night before. Now he and Cole were starving with hunger and shivering with cold. From time to time Raider cast an envious glance at the snoring miner.

The first station turned out to be a shack in which lived a stock tender, and a corral, where several fresh teams of horses looked out at them over the rails.

When the stock tender came out of the shack to meet them, Raider yelled at him, "Gimme plenty of ham and a double order of eggs."

The man looked back at him as if he were crazy. "I don't have no hens and pigs up here. Does this look like a restaurant to you?"

Raider was taken aback. "We was told we could get breakfast up here."

"Not unless you're willing to chew on hay or put your head in a bag of oats." The stock tender guffawed.

"Hell, you ain't gonna get nothing to eat on this route till nigh on sundown."

"Maybe later, if we get slowed by drifts," the driver shouted.

Raider sat in the coach and listened to his belly rumble, to Cole complaining of not having gone with Doc, and to the drunk miner snoring. The blizzard continued and the cold grew more intense. The fresh team of horses beat their way through the snow, the driver cussing at them all the while to keep himself warm. The snow blew in through chinks in the coach's woodwork and built up a half an inch on the floor. Cole Brent's teeth were chattering and his face was blue. Both he and Raider suspected that the miner had blankets inside a canvas roll on the rack, yet both would have frozen to death rather than go through a sleeping man's belongings.

Finally the cold and the shaking of the coach roused the sleeping miner. He reached up for his canvas roll and pulled a number of blankets from it. When he opened them he discovered that either he or some friend had wrapped two cold roast chickens and a bottle of whiskey in them. The miner couldn't bear to look at food the way he was feeling and gave his two fellow passengers a bird each, along with a blanket. He was less generous with his whiskey and went back to sleep with the half-empty bottle clutched tight to his chest.

Doc's train didn't arrive in Kelton that morning or that afternoon either. It was almost eight in the evening when its whistle blew and the lamp at the front of the locomotive showed way down the track. Doc loaded Judith and his wagon aboard a boxcar, made sure she had water to drink, oats to eat, and straw to lie on, then found his own compartment in the sleeping car. He did paperwork and read as the train roared across the darkness of Nevada. Last thing he remembered before falling asleep was the train stopping at Wadsworth, short of the California border, and thinking it a pity he was going to miss seeing the mountains because of darkness. When he woke next morning the train was still in Wadsworth. It had snowed overnight and the sagebrush plains looked desolate.

He asked a porter how much longer the delay would be.

"That depends on the snow, sir, not me. Could be anywhere from half an hour to three weeks."

Judith refused to leave the warmth and comfort of the boxcar, not feeling as strongly as her master about the benefits of exercise. Doc soon tired of stomping up and down on the thin crust of snow and flapping his arms to keep warm. He felt he daren't go into town in case the train pulled out while he was there, so he fetched from the wagon a bottle of dark rum—a tonic he often recommended for sluggish blood—and joined an all-day game of stud poker in the smoking car. When the train got under way once more, at seven that evening, he was about $50 ahead. He felt bad all over again that he was going to miss the mountains in the darkness, especially when they were covered with snow. The other players in the game didn't seem to give a damn.

The two locomotives labored as they pulled the train up into the Sierras. Every time the car door was opened by a trainman, billows of smoke filled the car, heavy with sulphur gas from the soft coal. Outside the windows, snowflakes whipped against the glass. The cold inside the car became intense. Doc was $90 ahead when the game was abandoned and everyone headed for his bed.

When Doc awoke it was broad daylight and he was sweating. From where he lay, he reached and pulled back the curtain covering the window. He was amazed to see orchards with flowering trees in the sunshine. The last time he had looked out it had been the dead of winter in the mountains. Here it was late springtime in California. The train stopped at a country station and Doc gazed out the window at pretty young things in summer dresses. He felt a strong urge to say to hell with Oregon and the Pinkerton Agency. He'd get off the train here, along with Judith and the wagon, and they'd never hear from him again in Chicago! But of course he stayed put, knowing he could never rest easy in his mind if he left his duty undone. Maybe after he finished in Oregon, he'd take some time off and spend it down here. He might even draw a case down this way. Maybe.

The Southern Pacific was now the Central Pacific, and the line ran from Sacramento by way of Stockton and Niles to Oakland. He spent one night in San Francisco and the next day boarded the steamship *City of Chester*, bound for Portland, Oregon, by way of Astoria, at the mouth of the Columbia River. Judith had to be lifted on board by a pair of slings under her belly. As she was hoisted into the air by the crane, she looked down at Doc in a mournful, accusing way.

"It's more the indignity of the thing than the discomfort she's feeling," Doc explained to a bystander on the dock, who looked at him strangely and moved away.

The mule stowed safely in the hold, Doc went to his cabin, which had berths besides his own. The voyage from San Francisco to Astoria was expected to take five days. The ship steamed north up the California coast-line, keeping the pine-covered shore in view off the starboard side. The sea was calm and blue. There was not a single cloud in the sky, and the ship's motion in the water was easy and pleasant.

Doc noticed her the first day out—standing alone on deck, her long scarf trailing in the sea breeze. He smiled, but she did not acknowledge his greeting.

An hour later he saw her in the dining salon, alone at a small table. He took a table near hers, so near he could smell the scent she used, which he thought might be jasmine. Although she was seated facing him, she never even glanced his way and did not appear to notice his presence throughout the meal. It was the same after-ward in various parts of the ship—so far as she was concerned, he didn't exist. Not used to this kind of treatment from a woman, Doc looked anxiously at him-self in mirrors, combed his hair often, and checked to make sure he was missing no buttons from his suit. He might as well have been invisible to her. Some male passengers did approach her. She cut them dead, and after that the others kept away. Women avoided her.

If Weatherbee had had anything to do, or if there had been other pretty unescorted women on board, he would not have become so intrigued by this woman. She was not young—probably in her early thirties, and defi-nitely an experienced woman of the world. She was beautiful in a sophisticated, perfect way, and although she never smiled, she wasn't sad. For two days she re-mained apparently totally unaware of the handsome, fashionably dressed Pinkerton who called himself a doctor. Surely she had some minor ailment for which he could provide balm. Weatherbee bribed a waiter to make sure word got to her that he was a medical man, but she showed no interest—the first woman Doc had known who was able to resist the temptation to discuss the ills that flesh is heir to. Then, for no apparent reason, at the end of lunch on the third day out, she glanced his way and met his eyes for a moment.

Doc needed no second bidding. He rose immediately and went to her table. She avoided his eyes as a smile spread across her face. She was not shy. This smile was unmistakably one of victory.

Doc decided he would be better off saying nothing rather than making silly remarks about how pleasant the voyage and weather were or how pleased he was to talk with her. She remained cool and collected, showing no inclination to open a conversation.

He reached beneath the tablecloth and placed a hand on her left knee. He could feel her shapely leg beneath her silk gown as his palm and fingers glided up her thigh and stroked her. The warmth of the smooth skin beneath came through the fabric.

She softy lifted his hand from her thigh and looked around the dining salon. The place was nearly empty by now, and the few still there were paying no attention to them.

"Cabin Eighteen," she said, then rose to her feet and walked away.

Doc lingered for five minutes over his coffee before he too left. Cabin 18 was in the section for first-class private cabins. He knocked at the door. She opened it, dressed in a long pink silk and lace gown, with her auburn hair hanging loose on her shoulders. He locked the door behind him and took her in his arms, kissing her and easing her voluptuous body out of its covering.

He laid her on the berth, where she stroked her breasts and body while she watched him undress.

The ship rocked slowly as Doc lay beside her. She placed her cheek on his belly and played with his rigid cock with one hand. Doc felt the sensitive tip of his member enter her feathery mouth. Her tongue snaked over the length of his cock and, frantic with lust, she sucked him greedily. Doc held back as long as he could, but her soft warm lips, tongue, and mouth sent such powerful charges of pleasure through him, he came in furious spasms which she swallowed into herself.

After a short rest, her hands caressed his member, and soon lust for her body made it swell upright again. Doc eased himself into her tight moistness and at first let the ship's motions set the pace of his lovemaking. Apart from her little cries and sobs of pleasure, he never heard her make another sound except for those two words she had spoken to him—"Cabin Eighteen."

He never learned her name. That evening in the dining salon she pretended not to see him, and again the next day.

CHAPTER THREE

At Durkee, in the valley of the Burnt River, about twenty-five miles short of Baker City, Raider decided to quit the stagecoach while the horses were being changed.

"We'd be best off not seen arriving together," he told Cole Brent. "From now on, you don't know me from Adam, nor Weatherbee either when he arrives. We're neither of us going to go around town claiming we're Pinkertons, 'cause nothing will get you a bullet in the back faster than that. There's a share of skunks in every town who'd like to settle a score with the Pinkertons, and they're not too particular about choosing which one. So you just keep your distance from us and keep your mouth shut and your eyes and ears open."

"I'll work on my own," Cole said huffily, obviously greatly disappointed he was not going to be hanging around Baker City with the two Pinkertons as his pards.

"You keep out of this, young'un," Raider snapped. "I'll see your father on the sly and find what I need to know from him. You keep your nose out of our affairs."

"And you stay out of mine!"

Raider saw he was taking the wrong approach. He would have to give Cole a job to do, so he could feel involved and not interfere where he wasn't wanted.

"We'll leave you to do what you should, so long as you get things done," Raider told him. "You have a house on that ranch of yours?"

"Sure."

"How far out of town is it?"

"Six, seven miles. It's called the Double T."

"You think you could hold off a bunch of guns from inside the house?" Raider asked.

"It'd need to be fixed up a bit. Put up shutters on the windows. Bring in food, water, ammo, and more long guns. Clear away some things. Could be done."

"We need a man to get it done," Raider said. "I'll see your father about it."

"Hey, what about me? How come you're cutting me out of everything? I ain't a kid. I can handle myself. Ain't no one knows that ranch as well as I do."

"Then you go ahead and take care of it," Raider said, as if he were giving in to him.

After the stagecoach was gone, Raider carried his carbine into the nearest saloon, propped it against the bar, and ordered a bottle of red-eye. He might as well enjoy it while he could. Soon enough Weatherbee would be around, criticizing the quality and demanding and lecturing. The trouble with Weatherbee was that he expected everybody to live up to his standards. He could never understand how Raider preferred to just go along with things as he found them.

"You looking for a job?" The question was asked by a beefy muscular man with small eyes spread far apart and fat cheeks.

"Maybe."

"Which side do you come down on? The sheep-herders or cattlemen?"

Raider grinned. "Which side is winning?"

The man's voice grew threatening. "Stranger, that may pass as a joke in other parts, but it ain't no joke around here."

Raider shrugged. "I make my jokes where and when I please. I haven't met up with the man yet who could decide me otherwise."

This caused the man to back down when he saw he was headed fast for trouble. "Well, I do have an answer to that question. The sheepmen is winning, if you count who has the most money to spend. You find more of them than you do cattlemen in the saloons and gaming house, so they seem to have the better of the argument. You see, they got a market close by for their wool. They ship it down the Columbia River to Portland or on to San Francisco. They're low-down dirty types. Us cowmen look down on sheepherders."

"Is there a market for mutton?"

"Hell no," the cattleman said. "Most folk here'd soon as eat a mule as a sheep. No, even the sheepherders eat beef. We got the finest bunch grass here, fattens them cows up like they never get in Texas—only tragedy is, we have nowhere to sell them. We have to drive them east to the railroads. We don't have a Chisholm Trail or the like of that up here. The cows just get drove wherever there's grass and water, heading east all the time until they meet up with some railroad town that has a stockyard. It ain't no way to market beasts and make some money. Then behind our backs we got them sheep chewing down the rangeland so there's nothing left but dirt. Us cowmen have to organize, get ourselves—"

Raider held up a hand. "I don't want any part of that."

"I hope you say that to the sheepherders, too."

"I will," Raider assured him.

They had a drink on that, and another. Pretty soon the talk got turned to the troubles going on in Baker City. The cattleman, whose name was Jason Wymes, said that he lived there. He cursed the mayor and the sheriff, saying they were out to rob everybody.

"You know a good place to stay if I go there?" Raider asked.

"Stay at Blind Danny's—it's the best. He's as much a crook as the mayor and sheriff, but he don't rob his hotel guests."

Wymes didn't say anything more about Daniel Brent, and Raider didn't want to press him for fear of arousing the man's suspicions. The cattleman went on at length about the sheriff gouging illegal taxes from the ranchers in the county and how he wasn't going to be forced to pay. In fact, he was supporting those who said the election had been faked, so the county seat would return to Spirit Lake, and the old sheriff, who bothered nobody, would be reinstalled.

"What the mayor of Baker City done is this," he explained to Raider. "He was elected by the thousand or so residents of that town, and outside that town he don't have no more authority than a grasshopper. So what does he do? He starts up a campaign to make Baker City the county seat, and he puts his own man in as sheriff. Now instead of controlling just one town he runs the whole county and has all the county taxes pouring in his back door. What's going on now is that the folks down at Spirit Lake won't part with the tax rolls and other paperwork he needs, and the sheriff is threatening to kick ass if they ain't handed over. Some people in Baker City tried to agree with the folk down at Spirit Lake, but a few of them got shot by drifters, who then escaped from town. That kind of quieted down the others. Hell, I think we should just string up the whole city council and have done with it. A lot of others think that way too, but thinking is one thing and doing is another."

"Well, I ain't going to ride against no sheepherders for you," Raider said, "but I don't mind giving you a hand if you have troubles with that crowd."

"I'll keep that in mind."

Raider went to an eating house and was served a plate of fried salmon, potatoes, and carrots. He bought a horse at the livery stables and a saddle at K. Brown & Son, Saddlemakers. The big bay gelding was manageable but needed new shoes. Raider left him at the forge, with instructions that he was to be left for him at the stables. This put going to Baker City out of the question for that day. Raider made a round of the saloons, and it was late before he bothered looking for a room at the hotel. They had none left. The place was built of logs and warm inside.

"Hell, I think it's too cold to sleep outside tonight, even if I do have a skinful of red-eye to keep me warm."

The hotel clerk jerked his thumb over his shoulder. "You go in our saloon there and when you feel like it you can sack out on the floor. I've one blanket left which I can rent you for a dollar."

"A dollar! That's highway robbery!"

The hotel clerk grinned. "Well, you can sleep on the floor without it, if you can. Or you can belly up to the bar all night if you think you can stay on your feet."

Raider paid and took the blanket. The hotel bar was a recent addition, a lean-to against the wall of the building made of rough planks. A number of men were already wrapped in blankets on the floor, asleep or trying to sleep in spite of shouts and singing from those still at the bar. Raider found himself a space next to a wall that seemed out of the main flow of things. As he tried to sleep a fight broke out at the bar. One man was knocked on top of some of the sleepers, and several of them threw off their blankets to beat him further. Last thing Raider remembered was an off-key rendering of "Suwanee River," and even that couldn't keep him awake.

After almost being tossed out of the upper berth of his cabin several times, Doc Weatherbee pulled on his clothes and a borrowed oilskin. He climbed a gangway to the deck and was immediately hit with salty spray. The ship lurched to and fro in the darkness, and he heard the waves crashing against its sides. He had to cling to a rail to brace himself against the wind as he made his way aft along the pitching, heaving deck.

He saw a sailor lashed with rope to the rail on either side of the stern. It was impossible to talk to the men because of the screaming of the wind and the slapping of water on the deck. They stood by tackle attached to the tiller, which Doc guessed was a standby in this weather should the wheel ropes break. Certainly if the ship went out of control and swung broadside into these waves they could easily flip it over. And lifeboats and swimmers could forget it out there in the raging dark of these storm-tossed seas.

Clinging to the rail, Doc made his way forward again to a gangway that led to the hold. Judith was doing all right, keeping her balance by splaying out all four legs. Doc wasn't sure what a seasick mule looked like, but she was a pretty good imitation of one. Again he received a mournful accusing look from her, like he had when she was being hoisted aboard, and again he felt guilty. He took some sugar lumps from his pocket and offered them to her. She refused. This was the first time she had ever refused a bribe of sugar. He could believe it now. This mule was no sailor.

Some human beings who were feeling much the same way as Judith were sitting white-faced in the smoking saloon. Doc ordered a beer and lit up an Old Virginia cheroot. He felt their eyes upon him, glaring at him with the resentment seasick people feel against those who enjoy themselves on any seas. Daylight was coming as a gray glare through the storm. A crewman told Weatherbee that they were waiting for enough light to steer past the bar at the river mouth. As soon as it was full day, the ship got under way once more. Inside the estuary, the wind died and rain came beating down in sheets. The ship tied up to the Astoria dock at eight A.M.

When Doc learned they would be there for several hours, unloading sheet tin for salmon cans, he put on the oilskin and tramped onshore in the rain. Astoria seemed to be built on piles in the water and consisted of sodden wood buildings separated from one another by mud and puddles.

"It's been raining here every day for a solid seven weeks now," a man told Doc in the tone of voice of someone boasting that he was worse off than anyone else. "Where are you bound for?"

"Baker City."

"Ah, that's back in the desert, I think."

"More up in the mountains."

He didn't pay any heed to Doc's correction. "Other side of the Cascades is dry as a bone, they tell me. I never seen for myself because I came up here by ship from Panama, which was in the days before there were trains that went from coast to coast. I took a ship from Baltimore down to Panama and walked across twenty-five miles of jungle to the Pacific. That's what I'd like to see some day."

"What?"

"A train. Oh, they had them in Baltimore before I left, but somehow I never saw one. I never wanted to. It's only when you're in a place like this that doesn't have them, that's when you really feel the need. How will you be traveling in the desert?"

"In the mountains," Doc said. "by mule and wagon."

"I hear they have mostly burros out there in them sandy plains. It's a real wonder to think of the Cascade Mountains splitting this state in two, one half wet and the other dry. I ain't talking about liquor now. The whole of Oregon is wet as any state in the Union. But this western half uses up all the rain, leaving them nothing but thorn bushes and stones. Know what they call us over there? Because it's so wet here. Webfoots. That's what they call us."

The ship journeyed upriver and tied up at Portland early the next morning. Doc unloaded Judith and the wagon, and they drove around Portland in the drizzle to celebrate being on more or less dry land again. The city extended along the bank of the Willamette River for about a mile and was six or seven blocks deep. Tree frogs chirped from the wet leaves of street trees, and green moss covered the shingled roofs.

Raider found that Baker City was mostly just one main street, with short side streets that soon died out. He discovered Blind Danny's place with no trouble from the large sign along one side of the building reading

MAJESTIC HOTEL. He took a room for a week. Daniel
Brent himself was equally easy to spot—a small man,
skin and bones, with a shock of white hair. He wore
wire-rimmed spectacles with blacked-out glass, but
apart from this, no one would have suspected he was
blind from the way he hurried about his hotel taking
care of things.

When he had a chance, Raider took him to one side,
"I'm one of the two Pinkertons. Name's Raider."

Brent smiled. "My son described you to me yesterday before he went out to the ranch. When you arrived
here today, my wife at first thought you were a gunman
—she describes everyone in detail to me. From what
my son had told me, I guessed it was you."

Raider had noticed the pretty woman sizing him up
earlier on, except that he had hoped it was for other
purposes, not supposing she was Cole's mother and
Daniel's wife.

"It seems you come here just in time," Brent went
on. "We had a blowup at the city council meeting this
afternoon. A young reporter, name of Keefe, ran off at
the mouth after he walked in on us without permission.
The newspaper owner is a buddy of the mayor, but he
won't be in any position to fire Keefe, because the reporter knows too much about some things going on at
the paper. Keefe reckoned the mayor will have him shot
for sure. He's been hiding in an empty room upstairs for
the past few hours. You think you can help him out? He
don't want to leave town if he doesn't have to."

Raider said, "I don't want this newspaperman to
know that I'm a Pinkerton. Them bastards always promise not to say a word, and next thing you know you're
reading about it on the front page."

"So don't tell him. As well as looking out for Keefe,

here's a list of things I want you to do."

"That ain't how we Pinkertons work, Brent," Raider told him. "If anyone's giving orders between us two, it's gonna be me. One thing you can do is cancel our arrangement anytime you please and I'll leave town and you can have things all your own way."

"You listen to me," Brent said. "I'm paying your salary. I brought you to this town. While you're here, you'll do what I say or I'll have Mr. Pinkerton send me someone more agreeable."

Somehow Raider had expected this blind man to be less aggressive than this; now he could see that a man with this drawback would have to be tough to prosper, or even survive, here in Oregon. The Pinkerton was angered, but he held back the words that came to his mind right away and instead calmly explained, "You don't pay my salary. You pay the Pinkerton National Detective Agency a retainer for two operatives to come here to clear your name and maybe clean up this town. I'm one of those operatives, and how I decide to go about saving your ass is going to depend on my judgment, not on yours. As for finding someone more agreeable, you had better send your boy back to Chicago with your complaint. Maybe you should go there yourself and stay awhile."

Brent was rigid with anger, yet he too stayed under control. His thatch of white hair bobbed like a quail's topknot as he began talking again. "I know this town, Mr. Raider. You're a stranger here. I know the ones who mean no good and I know which ones you can depend on—also the ones who go whichever way the wind blows. In practical terms, I can save you a lot of time if you'll listen to me instead of floundering around on your own."

"I'm sure I'll have a lot of questions to put to you, sir, as I start getting acquainted with the town." Raider's tone was polite. All the same, there was something in his voice which implied that some of these questions might be directed at Brent about his own doings. "You'll appreciate that your own involvement in these matters and your own strong viewpoint, which I've heard from your son, are just one side of the story. I want to hear the other side for myself."

"Who the hell do you think you are?" Brent bellowed, his small frame trembling with rage. "You think you're some kind of judge? Is that all my money gets me? Is this what I sent to Chicago for? Hell, no. I didn't send for someone to listen to the other fella's point of view—I sent for someone who'd listen to me and do what I want him to do."

"Then you should've gone down to a saloon and hired yourself some guns," Raider said. "They're cheaper than Pinkertons, and they don't ask awkward questions about your intentions."

"I'm a law-abiding man, Mr. Raider."

Raider was about to say "So am I" but changed it to "I try to be."

Keefe, the newspaper reporter, was in Room 9. Raider tried to get him to open the door, with no success. No answer—not a sound—came from the other side of the locked door. The Pinkerton had to fetch Brent and have him open the room door with a master key. They found Keefe standing in an empty closet with a derringer in his shaky hand. Brent calmed him down and then left.

"Mr. Brent was telling me about your awkward situation," Raider said. "I thought you had better tell me some more yourself. Maybe I can be of help. Get yourself out of this room and come out for a drink. It'll steady you down."

"I can't!" Keefe gasped. "They'll shoot me dead!"

"Being dead is more fun than hiding in a hotel room closet. Come on." Raider pushed him out into the corridor ahead of him.

Keefe was clearly as much in fear of the big Pinkerton as he was of whoever he imagined lay in wait for him outside. He had a pair of spectacles on his narrow face with the thickest lenses Raider had ever seen. He was about the same height and weight as Daniel Brent —about right for a jockey or Pony Express rider— though he was no more than thirty, while the hotelkeeper was in his fifties. Another big difference between them was that Brent walked confidently around like he could see, while Keefe moved nervously and hesitantly as if he were afraid of bumping into something hard and unseen.

Raider deliberately took him a good ways down the street before they went into a saloon. He wanted anyone who might be interested to get a good look. Keefe was gulping in air like a condemned man standing with a noose around his neck, just waiting for the trapdoor and eternity to open under his feet. He had no idea that this big ruffian was a Pinkerton. In his panicked way he half assumed Raider was someone Brent had paid to run him out of the hotel—although Brent had gladly offered him shelter earlier on and all he would have needed to do to get the reporter to leave was ask him to. But Keefe wasn't thinking too straight. Instead of being even halfway logical, he was worrying about bullets.

Raider pushed him through the doors of the Egyptian Palace, which had a large blue triangle, representing a pyramid, and a small white camel painted on the building's false front. Inside, there were glass-bead curtains, a hookah pipe nailed high on one wall, and behind the bar a large oil painting of a reclining lady whose only covering was a veil over the lower half of her face. Otherwise the decor was strictly native Oregonian— rough plank walls and floor, carelessly carpentered tables and chairs, a long bar with a brass footrail, men in flannel shirts and denims cursing, drinking, and laughing.

Raider sat Keefe down at a table some distance from the bar, where it was quieter and they could talk. When their bottle came, he poured four fingers of whiskey into Keefe's glass and ordered him to swallow it down. The reporter tried and failed to down such a quantity of the fiery liquid, but at least the effort to do so had a noticeable effect upon his outlook on life. He was soon jabbing his forefinger in Raider's chest and giving him the inside story on Baker City. Raider guessed that Keefe must also have had his nose in a glass before he interrupted the city council meeting earlier in the day.

Joe Keefe was the lead reporter for the Baker City *Sentinel-Advocate*. He had worked for a number of other papers, starting in San Francisco. "Bigger the city, the smaller my job. So I kept on hitting increasingly smaller towns and growing more important. I was a copy boy in San Francisco, I covered fruit and vegetables in Sacramento, politics in Spokane, until out here in Baker City I'm chief correspondent, with the world as my field. And I better keep writing about the outside world—because some of the other things I want to write about this town will never see print in the *Sentinel-Advocate*."

"You like the mayor?" Raider asked.

"He's scum. I'll give you an idea what he's like. He owns a mining brokerage firm here in town in a fifty-fifty partnership with my boss at the newspaper. They're the only mining brokers in town. So we produce two editions of our weekly paper—one giving factual information for home consumption, the other containing glowing accounts of rich strikes and fabulous mining activities. We ship all copies of that edition back east. The paper carries ads for the mining brokerage firm, who are only too willing to assist and advise any Easterners who might want to invest in a sure thing without having to make a tedious trip out here to the wilderness to see for themselves."

"You write both editions?"

"Sure do, not that I'm proud to admit it."

"I can see why some people might not want you to leave town in an unhappy frame of mind," Raider said.

Keefe's newfound confidence and energy suddenly evaporated. He looked warily around him and then scanned the faces at the bar as best he could across the room through his thick lenses. Raider poured him another drink, and this cheered him up some.

To change the subject, Raider said, "I met a cattleman out at Durkee yesterday. Jason Wymes."

Keefe grimaced. "Wymes thinks his shit don't smell because he's a big cattleman these days. They say he was run out of Kansas as a rustler. I once did a story on how he put his ranch together. Made him mad as hell. He said he was going to shoot me, and I was dodging into doorways and diving down alleys for weeks afterward when I'd see him walking toward me. But then came that inevitable day when we met face to face. I was preparing myself to meet my maker when he laughed, slapped me on the back, and bought me a drink in the nearest saloon."

"How did he put his spread together?" Raider asked.

"From bits and pieces. Although he and his family live here in town, he owns one of the biggest ranches in Baker County. He bought up land around springs and streams, acquiring forty acres in one place, a small tract somewhere else, a section of land along a creek bottom in another place. He built slowly by gaining control of the watering places. Now he owns maybe fifty or sixty parcels of land over a wide area, but because he controls the water, in effect he has the sole use of the vast government-owned ranges over much of the area. Only his cattle graze there, since only his cattle can find water to drink."

"He told me he was having trouble with the sheepherders."

Keefe laughed. "More like the sheepmen are having trouble with him. There hasn't been as much killings and destruction of animals in these parts as in some others, but there's been some bloodletting, and Jason Wymes's hands are far from clean. I can tell you another thing. If ever I wrote an article exposing vigilantes—which I expect I never will—Jason's name would figure high on the list of Vigilance Committee members. Some folk look to him to clean up the dirty work in town because the mayor is afraid of him."

"Wymes cussed out just about everybody, including the mayor and Daniel Brent."

"There's no harm in Danny," Keefe said quickly. "He's a town booster, and he's been taken advantage of by some unscrupulous people. But they underestimate Blind Danny. He's tough as boot leather and stubborner than a mule. Smart, too, though he likes to hide that. There's a lot of folk believe a man who can't see can't think. He lets them go on believing that. Which makes me kind of wonder what you and he have in common that makes him tell you to look after me."

Raider smiled at the newspaperman's instinct for a hidden story and knew better than to try to invent some kind of explanation. He allowed Keefe to ramble on about the town and the personalities in it, keeping the reporter's courage up with liberal doses of spirits, while he himself drank hardly at all and waited for trouble to show its face.

Raider never did find out what exactly Keefe had said at the city council meeting that had got the mayor so riled at him. Raider wasn't too interested in details right now—he just wanted to see the big picture. He wasn't sure he was even getting that, since everyone he had spoken with so far had his own ax to grind. Joe Keefe was going to be a problem. The man was a drunk and physically useless as a fighter. He didn't even wear a gun. Best Raider could think of was to provide him with safe passage out of town after Weatherbee arrived, and to hide him in the meantime out with Cole Brent at the ranch. He told none of this to Keefe, because he didn't want to hear the reporter's opinions on it. When the time came, he would tell Keefe what to do, and Keefe would do it or look out for himself in the future. He was not going to be a millstone tied to Raider's neck, dragging him down.

Right now Keefe was going nowhere. Raider had use for him—to help him make contact with the other side's hired guns, kick up a little dust, and see who was who.

He didn't want them to know he was a Pinkerton, but he did want them to know he was someone they had to reckon with. The sooner they recognized that, the better for everyone concerned.

It wasn't too long before five men came in the door. One of them looked sideways in their direction, said something to the other four, and went out into the street again. The remaining men walked across the saloon toward their table.

"That was Fredericks who left after pointing me out," Keefe said urgently. "He owns the *Sentinel-Advocate*. These men are going to shoot me."

Raider grabbed his arm so he couldn't jump up and run away. "Listen to me, Keefe. I can't handle these four if they're expecting trouble. If they ask you, go with them and create no fuss. Just before you reach the street door, hit the man nearest you as hard as you can and then drop to the floor."

Keefe's face was a picture of dismay and betrayal. All along Raider had been promising to protect him. He would never have left Blind Danny's place at all if this big lug hadn't forced him to. Now, first threat that came along, he was being asked to surrender quietly. But Keefe had no time for arguments or recriminations. The four men had reached their table and were standing there looking down at them. They were a mean bunch —raggedy, dirty, grim-faced.

"Joe Keefe?" one of them asked.

"What is it to you, mister?" the newspaperman snapped back, with more guts than Raider had credited him with.

"We need you to step outside with us. A private matter."

"What if I don't want to go?" Keefe asked.

"No need to take that attitude. You ride with us a ways so we have a chance to talk."

The four men were watching Raider more than they were watching Keefe. The Pinkerton pretended not to want any part of what was going on—he was a stranger in town and couldn't be expected to involve himself in Keefe's problems. But the four men couldn't be certain, and they watched for the big man to make a move, any move, ready for him.

The reporter emptied his glass, nodded to Raider, and stood to leave with the men. Just before they reached the exit, Keefe swung his fist into the gut of the man nearest him. It wasn't much of a punch, its main impact coming more from surprise than force, but it worked. The man gasped, doubled over, and clutched his stomach. Keefe fell to the floor at their feet, and one of the others pulled back his right foot to boot the prone newspaperman. He stopped in mid-kick when he heard a revolver being cocked behind him. All went for their guns.

Raider had six loaded chambers and four armed opponents. And a small advantage in time. He shot the nearest man to him—about fifteen paces away—while that man's hand was just touching his gun handle. The bullet slapped into a leather vest he had on, but this wasn't enough to stop the flight of the lead projectile nearly a half inch in diameter. It tore through the vest, and the shirt and skin beneath it, broke a rib, and cut through his liver as though it was butter.

He was still staggering on his feet when Raider thumbed back the hammer of his Remington .44 and squeezed off a second shot, not at him but at the man next to him, who had his gun more than halfway out of its holster. The shot was high, and the bullet shattered the man's bony face. Instantly dead, he hit the floorboards before the man shot previous to him.

The Remington's hammer was snapped back again and its deadly barrel sought out its third victim. This was the man who had been about to kick Joe Keefe on the floor. He had his own gun about ready to fire, but the barrel was not leveled true on Raider yet. The Pinkerton kept his shot lower this time, catching the kicker low in the belly or in the groin. The man howled in pain and clutched at his wound with the blood-spattered fingers of his left hand and he slowly bent over.

It would have been too much for Raider to hope he would get the drop on all four of them through Keefe's tactic, but at least he had hoped that Keefe's blow would have slowed if not canceled out the fourth man. Such was not the case. The puny reporter's punch to the gut had distracted all four men, but the gunplay soon made the man he had hit forget about the light punch he had received. He was faster than his three pards and now had his .45 leveled at Raider, hammer cocked, finger on trigger, coolly eyeing for a sure shot at fifteen paces or so. Raider took in all this in an instant and knew he was too late to stop him, too late and too big to duck out of the way.

Prepared for the worst, Raider was amazed to see the man's face suddenly twist in pain and see him hop on one foot. He had been kicked on the shin by Keefe. The hammer on Raider's Remington fell on the firing pin, and the bullet launched itself from the barrel and buried itself in a shapeless mass of lead in the gunman's chest cavity.

Keefe pushed aside a blood-soaked body and sat upright on the floor. He adjusted his spectacles and looked around him. Then he hightailed it out the door.

CHAPTER FOUR

Doc Weatherbee was surprised by the large size of the stern-wheeler steamer he boarded for the trip upriver from Portland. He was in for more surprises as the huge Columbia River ran between terraced palisades on both banks. Some of these palisades were two thousand feet high, and most of them were covered with a wild tangle of vegetation. Streams fell hundreds of feet down the sides of cliffs. This was how Doc imagined the Amazon, certainly not what he expected in Oregon.

The stern-wheeler reached the Cascades in the afternoon, and its passengers and freight were loaded onto a narrow-gauge railroad to bypass the rapids. Doc loaded his wagon with difficulty onto a small flatcar, and Judith with even more difficulty in a miniature boxcar—she had never given him trouble with a regular train, always being pleased not to have to walk or haul, but she wanted nothing to do with this toy train. The track length was no more than three miles, and Doc was told that this was the only railroad as yet in the state. Doc wondered if the man at the Astoria dock who had never seen a train had heard about this one, or whether perhaps he wouldn't consider this little contraption the genuine article.

A military blockhouse was pointed out to him as having being built by General Sherman just after the Civil War.

"Well now, that's the first thing I ever heard of that was built by Sherman," a man with a strong Southern accent said. "Know what we call "'Sherman's tooth-picks'" down in Georgia? The brick chimneys left standing after his troops burnt the houses."

An uneasy silence followed this. A lot of Southerners had come to the Northwest after the war, and a fair share of Yankees, too. There were some who weren't willing to let old differences rest, even out here. But most had enough on their hands with survival in this harsh new land of Oregon; they had no wish to burden themselves further with quarrels brought from home.

Above the rapids, the passengers and freight went aboard another stern-wheeler, this one much smaller than the first. They steamed upriver as far as The Dalles, where the Columbia shrank from a width of three-quarters of a mile to only 150 yards. The water burst through this narrow gap in a rock formation with much the same force as Doc had seen in the Niagara Falls, except that here there was no waterfall, only a huge forceful flow.

Weatherbee hitched Judith to the wagon and drove through The Dalles to where he could get another boat upriver. This boat was still smaller, and the river itself was narrower in these upper reaches, though still a mighty waterway. Sandy plains now stretched away on either bank. The Cascade Mountains were behind, to the west, and among them Doc saw Mount Hood, rising high above everything else, cone-shaped and snow-capped.

The boat nosed into the bank at various places and

crewmen unloaded freight. The boxes and bundles were just left on the sand and the boat steamed off upriver. Doc could see no houses or any signs of settlement. Farther upriver he saw some Indians on the riverbanks, but when the boat nosed in and freight was unloaded near them, they remained sitting on their ponies or squatting on the ground, indifferent.

"Who is this stuff for?" Weatherbee asked a crewman.

"Ranchers. You don't see no houses because they're located on the hay bottoms of creeks and there's almost always some low hills between the river and them. Some mighty big spreads in these parts too. Some of the big ranches north of the river have more than twenty thousand head. The cattlemen will come collect their stuff in their own good time."

"They're not worried about the Indians taking it?"

"There used to be some misunderstandings on that score before the Nez Percé uprising back in '77, in which the Indians came out second best. Since then it's been considered good manners for the Indians to leave things alone on the riverbank. I ain't at all sure what they're thinking, and I guess it spooks us when they just stand there like we don't exist."

It was near dusk when Weatherbee left the boat at Umatilla. He spent the night at a hotel in town and left the next day at the crack of dawn on the trail to Hermiston. From there he would continue southeast through Pendleton and La Grande on to Baker City. The trail was slow going through the sand waste and the rolling plains of light, ashen soil. As the trail climbed higher, the country gradually changed. Fir, pine, cedar, spruce, and larch grew on the high mountain ridges. Cottonwood and willow fringed the creeks. The river bottoms were all ranchland. Out on the rangelands, cattle or sheep grazed, sometimes mixed, more often not. Mine tailings high on slopes and diggings in placer gravels were plentiful, and Doc was told that alluvial gold was still plentiful and also gold and silver quartz-leads.

Doc could feel himself getting closer by the moment to the troubles in Baker City. He wondered what Raider might be doing.

Raider dug his spurs into his horse's sides, bent low as he could get in the saddle, and cantered full speed down the middle of Baker City's main street. The two horsemen ahead of him maintained the distance between them and him by riding hellishly, glancing back over their shoulders. Raider swore at them and at his own horse and did everything he could to gain on them. He saw the faces of townspeople flash by, he saw men waving their arms, he rode his horse flat out, trying to squeeze every last ounce of speed out of him—but it was no good, he was too heavy, his horse wasn't fast enough, he couldn't close the distance between him and the riders ahead. They both crossed the finishing line ahead of him. Raider spat the dust from his mouth and wiped it from his eyes as he slowed his horse. He had come in third in a seven-horse race and dutifully handed over his five-dollar gold piece to the winner. At least, apart from the race stake, he hadn't bet on himself, but then most riders who are six foot two and more than two hundred pounds don't.

"I guess this nag ain't as all-fired good as I thought he was at the Star Saloon last night," Raider said.

"Ain't nothing wrong with that horse," the winner told him. "It was the man on his back who lost that race."

It was said in fun, and Raider took it that way. The winner was a cowhand for Jason Wymes. He was a light, bowlegged man, a natural horseman, whom no one bet against in a race except in a saloon late at night. Actually the big bay gelding Raider had bought at Durkee had done well in the race considering the load it had to carry and the fact that there was no handicapping, so that the light man had the greater advantage.

As Raider wiped down his sweating horse, a female admirer came by.

"Raider, I hate you!" the pretty woman said. "You made me lose a dollar! I was certain you would win!"

He laughed and pointed first to his spurs and then to his horse's sides. The animal was the only one without a bleeding hide. "I ain't cruel enough to use Oregon spurs," he said.

"Then I don't mind losing my dollar," she said, "so long as you treat me to a drink." She glanced at the heels of some of the riders around, whose spurs jangled loud as sleighbells. "I never saw such awful things anywhere else."

"Me neither."

The Oregon spurs had a shank and crotch of brass, and the rowel was about three inches in diameter and made from the steel blade of a handsaw. Two jangles, attached to the pinions on the outside of each spur, struck the rowel at every movement of the wearer's foot.

They walked down the street hurriedly, before the next race got under way, to put Raider's horse back in the stables. On their way back, one man standing with a group said to Raider, "Still in town? I thought you'd have moved on by now."

"I've no reason to," Raider said.

"We'll see by and by," the man responded.

The woman's name was Valerie, and she was a faro dealer Raider had met at the Star Saloon, where they went now.

"Why did the mayor say that to you?" she asked. "Because of the shooting?"

"I guess. He and Fredericks, the newspaper owner, tried to have the marshal arrest me, but I had Joe Keefe for a witness and the others in the saloon, so the marshal could see no cause. The mayor cussed him out and said he'd get the sheriff to do it when he next came to town, whenever that's going to be. I suppose he thought that would be enough to make me leave town."

"Where's Joe Keefe?" she asked.

Raider gave her a quick look. "I told him to ride out of here while he had the chance, since it was his own boss who put those four guns onto him. He didn't need much persuading."

"You know where he went?"

"You a friend of Joe's?"

"Sure," she said.

"He's safe."

She didn't persist in her questions any further. It wouldn't have got her anywhere if she had. Raider had found Keefe back hiding in Blind Danny's place after the shooting, and that night he rode out with him to the ranch house and left him in Cole Brent's charge. The mayor and Fredericks had been careful to avoid a direct confrontation with Raider, and he hardly knew either man. For their part, they had seen him talk with Jason Wymes in town, and if they got to wondering who Raider might have ties to, it would be with Wymes, not Daniel Brent.

• • •

Sheriff Nate Cahoon rode with his eleven deputies into the town of Spirit Lake. He had hired eight of the men a few hours previously at five dollars for the day. They were mostly cowpokes between jobs, and since they could expect to earn not much more than thirty dollars for a month's work on a ranch, from sunup to sundown, five dollars for a day's riding as a sheriff's deputy seemed like a paid holiday to them. They weren't gunmen, but everyone had had a few drinks and didn't mind plugging any bastard who stood up to them. After all, for this one day, *they* were the law.

The sheriff saw a freight wagon with high sides and back that looked empty by the way the team of four horses easily hauled it. He raised his hand for the driver to stop.

"What you carrying there?" the sheriff asked.

"I'm on my way to a store to load flour, salt, sugar, and sides of bacon for the mining camps outside town."

"You ain't anymore," the sheriff told him. "Baker County has need of this wagon for today, and I'm commandeering it in the county's name."

The driver shouted, "Why, you crazy young scamp!" and his hand dropped to the shotgun at his side. But then he saw the horsemen's hands drop to their revolver handles, so he left the shotgun where it lay and jumped down to the ground. "You're going to hear all about this, Cahoon. You don't have the power to do a thing like this unless it's an Indian attack or a flood or something like that. I'm going to see to it your badge is took off you."

"Sure you are," the sheriff sneered at him and then directed two of his deputies to climb aboard the wagon after tying their horses to its rear. The wagon and horsemen moved along Spirit Lake's one street, leaving the dispossessed driver standing red-faced and cursing in the dust behind them.

Nate Cahoon was enjoying himself. He had often enough got his ass kicked and been put in the drink tank overnight in this place. Now he was riding into town as the sheriff of Baker County, and he was going to show some of Spirit Lake's leading citizens the same kind of treatment they had shown him when he was a ranch hand. He had been in his early twenties then. At thirty-one, he could look back on those times and see himself as a good-natured kid who had let himself be pushed around by those no better than he was. The years had changed him a lot, Nate liked to say. He didn't go into particulars about what he had been doing that had brought about the change in him, although some said he had been a road agent. He had been a guard in some mining camps, and marshal of a small town up Pendleton way for a while.

Cahoon had done some favors for Baker City's mayor, and then was brought in by him to run for sheriff in the county election that changed the county seat from Spirit Lake to Baker City. He liked the mayor. Nate Cahoon recognized the fact that he himself was no great thinker. Things tended to go skewways when he planned them. What he needed was a thinker, a man with a talent for looking ahead—and the mayor for sure was that. The man could act also, as well as think. Between the two of them, they could control the county like it was their own backyard.

"This way, boys," the sheriff shouted, pulling his horse toward an alley between two stores. At the back of the stores stood a windowless warehouse with a large sliding door that was half open. Several men could be seen inside moving sacks around. "Is the boss here?" Cahoon asked one worker.

The man nodded and went to get him.

The boss came and scowled at Cahoon. The sheriff recognized his son with him. Neither was armed. There was a second son, called Mike.

"Mike not here?" Cahoon asked. "He should hear this."

"Mike!" the boss bellowed back into the warehouse, and then, while waiting for his other son to arrive, he looked suspiciously from the freight wagon to the sheriff and back. "Any merchandise you buy here, Cahoon, you pay for in gold coin here, before anything's loaded on that freighter."

"That ain't no problem," Nate said.

"There's a problem?"

"Sure there's a problem."

Mike arrived. He wasn't wearing a gun.

"All three of you will do me a big favor by climbing up into that wagon," the sheriff said politely. "Then we can discuss our problem."

Obviously thinking they were involved in some dispute about goods from their warehouse, the father and two sons stepped up on the rims of the wagon wheels and climbed over the sides. Standing inside the wagon, only their heads and shoulders showed above the sides. Cahoon nodded to the two men on the driver's bench. The driver flicked the lines and pulled to the left to turn around. The wagon started moving.

"Hey! Where the hell are you taking us?" the puzzled boss wanted to know. "This here wagon is empty! What's going on?"

"You're under arrest," Cahoon shouted. "I'm taking

you in to Baker City for trial on a conspiracy charge. Conspiring to foment disorder. Any one of you tries to jump out or even climb up on the sides of that wagon, he's a dead man. These men here have standing orders to shoot if you try something."

"You'll never get away with this, Cahoon!" the boss shouted. "You and the mayor of Baker City ain't got Judge Hayes in your pocket. He'll put you in your place!"

The sheriff only grinned at this. They were back on the street again, and he pointed to everyone to turn right. "We got some more no-account troublemakers to pick up."

They caught the next two men by surprise, both storekeepers behind their counters. People stood and stared in the street as the wagon with five men in it lumbered on, escorted by the sheriff and his deputies.

"This is like what they did in the French Revolution when they took Marie Antoinette and those others to the guillotine," one of the storekeepers said with a nervous titter.

The four other men in the wagon had no idea what he was talking about.

The group stopped outside a one-room log cabin next to the livery stables corral.

"You in there, Powell?" the sheriff shouted.

The door opened partway. "What do you want, you conniving skunk?"

"I got these men in the wagon here," Cahoon said. "I need to talk with you."

"No you don't," the voice said from behind the door. "If it had been an honest election, I'd still be sheriff of Baker County, not you. Fraud got you that tin star.

That's all I have to say to you, so take yourself out of here."

"I'm arresting you, Powell. Come on out here with your hands empty if you know what's good for you."

The door swung open fully and the double barrels of a scattergun poked out. The first blast blew Nate Cahoon out of the saddle and caused his horse to bolt. The second blast blinded those horsemen nearest the cabin, but the others farther back sent a volley of revolver shots into the open doorway.

The scattergun fell on the ground outside the doorway. Then Powell toppled out and fell face down, riddled with bullets.

Cahoon climbed to his feet with a smile on his face. "Watch that wagon. Make sure none of them get away. It was only birdshot. I ain't hurt." He touched his fingers to some of the red spots like pimples on his face and grimaced. "You fellas cut up?"

Two of the men were peppered with birdshot, though not as badly as Cahoon. He promised each of them a bottle along with their pay, and they quit complaining. After his horse had been fetched back, the sheriff said, "Come on. We have more work to do."

Tom Turnbull had turned fifty and now had more gray than black strands in his bushy hair. His mouth never fully closed on his misshapen, broken teeth, and a network of thin red veins showed on his cheeks and nose. His gaze made people nervous. In spite of his lack of good looks and charm, Turnbull had been elected mayor of Baker City. He was known throughout the northeastern part of the state as an accountant and financial administrator. As a young man he had received

training in a Philadelphia business college and had come
west to keep accounts for a big mining concern. No one
had ever spoken a word against him until after he had
become mayor, and there were many who believed that
the charges made against him were more based on jeal-
ousy than reality; when a man rises in the world, he
always has his detractors, who will not be satisfied until
he has lost everything he had gained.

Turnbull could be simple and direct. He said to
Homer Fredericks, owner of the Baker City *Sentinel-
Advocate,* "I put in thirty years of my life keeping watch
over other people's money and end up with next to
nothing in my own bank account. I might as well have
gone gambling and whoring and drinking like any cowhand for all I have to show for three decades of hard
work."

Fredericks nodded sympathetically and did not mention that, in his view, Turnbull had done more gambling, whoring, and drinking than any twenty cowhands
put together, since they only did it when they came in
off the range, while Turnbull was at it all the time.

"You can't blame me for wanting to put something
aside," Turnbull went on. "I'm getting on, and I have to
think of the years ahead. It's all right for these young
fellas who think they're going to last forever, or the
ones who don't expect to see thirty. Hell, I never
thought I'd see fifty. It's late, but finally I've gotten
around to thinking about myself. What do I get out of
all this? Do I end up with a sore back and an empty
pocket?"

Homer Fredericks was tempted to say that if Turnbull's back was sore, it was not from bending over his
account books for hours—more likely it was from
humping ladies. But all Fredericks did was nod. In his

opinion, every man had a right to feel sorry for himself now and then. Even if he didn't deserve to. Fredericks was also used to Turnbull going into long streams of self-justification before he did something of doubtful merit. He did all his talking before. After he had done it, he never opened his mouth about it again.

"You're fortunate, Homer, being a financially independent man all your life," Turnbull said. "I've had to struggle for every crust my family had to eat."

This was too much, even for Fredericks. "I've known you on and off for more than twenty years, Tom, and I must say you've hidden your hard times and poverty from us all."

"I've always spared my friends," Turnbull said piously.

Fredericks laughed. He was a big heavy man with a fleshy face, and he was strong as an ox. He knew that Turnbull's first wife had drowned herself and that his second wife had left him. They couldn't take his hell-raising ways and poor treatment of them.

Once Fredericks laughed in his face, Turnbull stopped talking about his misfortunes. He couldn't afford to take offense at Fredericks. The man was too important. And powerful. Instead he switched his talk to the business at hand.

"Nate Cahoon has most of the troublemakers in Spirit Lake lodged in the jail beneath the new courthouse here in Baker City. He brought them in about an hour ago. They killed Powell."

"Good riddance," Fredericks said.

"That's what I say. I was hoping Nate would kill some more of them—he's such a dumb bastard. But he didn't. The more he kills and the deeper we get him involved, the more he works for me."

"You?" Fredericks inquired.

"You too, Homer," Turnbull hastily assured him. "What we don't want is Nate getting the idea that *he* runs the county instead of us. He's already made a few cracks about him being elected countywide, while I'm only elected for Baker City. Best way for us to cut him down to size is have him do the dirty work. Then he has nowhere to go except stick with his friends. He doesn't have the brains to go it alone, and he's just about clever enough to realize it."

Fredericks looked at the sun, which was getting ready to set. "We should be on our way, Tom. I won't rest easy until we get this thing done."

It was the mayor's turn to laugh now, at the newspaper owner's unease. "Don't worry about a thing, Homer. Nate has cleared the way for us. There ain't much resistance left in Spirit Lake tonight. They're all chewing on jail food below our courthouse. The judge is on a roaring drunk, and it'll be late tomorrow before they get him thinking straight again. After we're done in Spirit Lake, that little shithead reporter of yours, Keefe, won't have a scrap of evidence to back up whatever fool story he wants to write about us. No one is going to publish it without some kind of evidence to back up his charges. Be simpler to shoot the little turd, if only we knew where he went. But once we get this done, he can't hurt us."

"I think we should be moving out," Fredericks insisted. "It's a good three hours' ride to Spirit Lake."

"Let it get dark. I don't want no one seeing my face while I'm headed that way."

The mayor, Fredericks, and four others who had reason to be interested met at the big rock outside the town, where the trail north split two ways. They took the

right-hand fork and made good time after it was fully
dark by the light of a new crescent moon and the bright
stars in the clear sky. Spirit Lake, being a quiet place,
had closed up for the night.

The six men spoke in whispers to each other, building one another's confidence, as their horses padded
quietly toward the town's dark and deserted street:

"Cahoon took out Powell earlier on today. They
never did have a marshal here because the county sheriff
lived in his cabin down by the stables. They never
thought to get anyone or make Powell marshal after he
lost the election. So we don't have nothing to worry
about there."

"The sheriff arrested and took in just about the whole
town council and most of those likely to give a damn.
This will be like taking candy from a baby."

"Ain't no one with a steady gun hand and a pair of
balls in this town anyhow."

"Better pull our bandannas up over our faces."

"One man stays with the horses. The rest go inside."

They all knew the location of the old courthouse.
The place had been built in a rush more than twenty
years before, and now it was falling to pieces. Its deter-
iorated condition and the lack of concern about this
among the citizens of Spirit Lake were two of the rally-
ing points Turnbull had used to gain support in his drive
to bring the county seat to Baker City. He had even
persuaded Blind Danny Brent to foot the bill for the new
courthouse in Baker City. The people in Spirit Lake
hadn't even bothered to try minor repairs on their building. The records were stored at the back.

One man stayed with the horses, out of sight in the
wasteland behind the courthouse. Turnbull inserted the
blade of his bowie between the window sashes and

flipped the catch open. He raised the lower part of the window and climbed inside. The four others followed with the saddlebags.

Over the years, Turnbull's duties as accountant and clerk for local mining firms had brought him many times to the county courthouse records. He knew where the papers were to be found when the person in charge didn't. He knew now where to go for what he wanted. He pulled open drawers of files, peering at them hardly at all, occasionally holding up a sheaf of papers to the window to examine them by moonlight. Some drawers he left open, others he pushed shut.

He pointed to the potbellied stove against one wall. "You three start burning the contents of every drawer I've left open. You gotta crush every paper into a ball before you throw it in. One sheet not burned all the way could be enough to send one of us to jail for a good many years. Or worse. We're all in this together, so don't worry which papers apply to who. We don't have time to sort through for what don't apply to us either. Just burn the lot. You can see there's way too much for us to carry. Make sure every bit burns. Homer, you come with me. Most of the papers we need are over this way. We ain't going to bother with births and deaths and such stuff. We need the county papers, land deeds, court papers, federal things. I'll pick. You stuff them in the saddlebags."

The men worked quietly and quickly. Their eyes had become accustomed to the dark on the long ride here. Soon a paper fire roared inside the stove, and the flames cast flickering light through the open stove door on the arms of the men pitching in crumpled papers.

"Fire! Fire!"

They heard the yell in the street outside. Someone

had smelled smoke coming from the dark building and was raising the alarm. The smoke was going out the chimney, but no doubt this could not be seen from the street in the darkness and the alarm raiser just assumed that the empty, disused building must be on fire.

"Keep burning them damn papers!" Turnbull hissed. "I'd like to have set fire to this place, but we need these records. We'll gain them all eventually. We're nearly finished over here. How's it going with you?"

"Slow. I thought paper would burn faster than this."

"Keep at it," the mayor said.

There were sounds of more voices outside, and someone was shaking a hand bell.

"I hope Clem don't lose his nerve and leave with the horses," Fredericks muttered.

"He better keep on going if he does," Turnbull said, "because I swear to God I'll put a bullet between his eyes if I find him in Baker City."

"Clem ain't going anywhere," another man said. "He's in this just like the rest of us. His name is on these papers just as much as mine."

That calmed them down, and they hurried on with their work, not heeding the growing commotion outside the building. Lamps carried by hurrying men cast yellow areas of light on the walls of the room. It would be only moments now before someone finally looked in and saw them—or at least noticed the glow from the open stove door.

But that was not what happened. The townspeople all ran to the front of the courthouse. Someone unlocked the door. Then men with lamps and others with buckets of water ran from the hearing room into the judge's chambers to the jury room and elsewhere, searching for the flames that had given rise to the smoke. The door to the room where the records were kept was thrown open. A man stood in the doorway, holding a lamp high, with several others behind peering over his shoulders.

"Who are you?" he shouted. "What are you doing here?"

The sound of the pistol shot was deafening in the high-ceilinged room. The man sagged and crumpled. His lamp crashed to the floor, shattering its glassed dome. The men behind him scattered into the dark, abandoning their fallen comrade.

Turnbull rushed to the door with his smoking Colt and fired five shots into the interior of the building. He listened with satisfaction to the panic this caused as men strove with one another to get out the front door of the building onto the street. He stamped out a small flame flickering on some spilled oil from the lamp, stepped over the body of the man, and stood near the window to reload his gun by moonlight.

The others, who had stopped burning papers in order to watch, hurriedly went back to their task. Fredericks, having dragged the six pairs of loaded saddlebags to the window, had joined the other three men in feverishly crumpling paper and tossing it in the stove door.

"I pray to God that Clem's still waiting with those horses," he said in a high nervous whining voice, which sounded odd coming from such a large, powerfully built man.

Turnbull said nothing, only gazed out the window and spun the reloaded chambers of his revolver.

Finally the four men's frantic efforts paid off. All the papers from the open drawers had gone up in flames. The mayor left the window and checked for himself that everything had been removed from the files and then looked into the stove to make sure everything was burning properly. He was in no hurry, in spite of the fact that a crowd was building outside by the sounds they could hear.

"Last time I heard people gathering up like that was for a lynching," Homer Fredericks observed gloomily.

Turnbull laughed scornfully. "Any hanging done tonight in Spirit Lake is going to be done by us. Maybe if we were to string up one of them, it'd chase the rest of them home fast—like they was walking on top of one another trying to get out the front door when I fired those shots."

"There ain't nothing but yella skunks left in this town," another man said. "Cahoon saw to that."

They all laughed and headed for the window. Following the mayor's orders, one man jumped outside and ran quickly to where they had left Clem with the horses. As he disappeared into the shadows, some gunshots followed.

"They're shooting at us!" Fredericks shouted. "We're trapped!"

"Easy down there, Homer," the mayor told him, as if he was a spooked horse.

He had the men throw the saddlebags out the window and then wait inside for a signal from the men with the horses.

"We go out one by one," Turnbull announced. "As he goes, each man grabs a pair of saddlebags. Homer, you're a big son of a bitch—you take a pair of bags in each hand. Mount your horses, stay back out of sight, and wait for everyone to come out. Every man try to pick off the shooters—or just fire on them so they can't aim good. We'll all be as safe as you like, only I want to show these Spirit Lake backwoodsmen they can't fire on Baker City men."

They heard a shout. The horses were ready. Clem had stood his ground. The first man rolled quickly out the window, landed on his feet, stooped to grab a pair of saddlebags bags, and made it as fast as he could out of the moonlight into the darkness beyond. A dozen shots rang out, and he was lucky to make it without being hit.

"The saddlebags slow us down," Fredericks said. "He made it only because he took them by surprise. They'll be waiting on the rest of us, and they won't miss next time."

Turnbull saw the truth of this and didn't try to argue. There were three men still inside and five pairs of saddlebags on the ground outside. The two men who had to carry two pairs of bags each would be further hampered. Since the mayor reckoned he would be one of those, for once he was willing to take Fredericks's complaint seriously. He walked back into the hearing chamber and looked out other windows to find an alternative escape route. One way out seemed no better than another. It was impossible to tell in the dark. The snipers could be anywhere, waiting for them to step into a clear patch of moonlight. He froze when he detected a movement.

It was in a window of the house across the alley. The lower half of the window was raised and someone was standing there watching. Turnbull reached for his gun, intending to plug this marksman. Then his eyes made sense of the movement. It was not one person. There were two. Kids. Two little girls standing side by side, with their heads and shoulders showing above the windowsill.

He quietly raised the courthouse window, then suddenly leaped out and crossed the dark alley in a couple of bounds. As he got close, he saw that the girls, no more than eight or nine, were twins and had identical

pairs of braids. Neither one moved, like rabbits mes-
merized by a weasel. By the time they thought to move
back, Turnbull had grabbed each by a braid. They were
small and light, and he yanked them out the window,
scratching and screaming. Holding on to each by a
braid, he dragged them around behind the courthouse
and displayed them in front of him.

"Shoot, you fuckers!" he yelled at the dark buildings.
"You'll probably hit one of these twins. I don't know
their names and I don't care. Maybe you can't tell one
from the other, so you won't know which one your bullet hit."

There was no gunfire during this speech, or after it.
Fredericks came out the window and took four pairs of
saddlebags, two pairs in each hand, while Turnbull
jerked the kids around by their hair to provide cover.
Fredericks made it into the darkness safely. That left one
man still inside the courthouse, and one pair of saddlebags lying on the ground outside the window.

Turnbull could hear the horses stamping just a short
distance away. "Come on," he called to the last man
inside. "What's keeping you?"

The man climbed out the window. At that moment,
the twin whose braid Turnbull held in his right hand
twisted her head around and bit his hand. The other one
stamped her heel on the toe of his left boot. They broke
out of his clutches and scooted down the alley.

"Little bitches!" Turnbull roared. "Vixens!"

The man coming out the window took a bullet in the
middle of his chest and another high in his right
shoulder. He fell backward into the courthouse.

Turnbull grabbed the remaining pair of saddlebags
and tried to cross the moonlit area for the darkness
beyond, where the horses waited. A hail of fire drove

him back. Lucky not to be hit, he slunk back against the courthouse wall, next to a downpipe in a corner. For the moment he was hard for them to see, and he waited for an opportunity to dash across the open space again.

But the townsmen had tasted blood, and they wanted more of it. They had hit one of the raiders and they had another trapped. They intended not to lose him, especially since he was the one coward enough to hide from bullets behind children. Some of them decided to rush him.

As soon as they hit the moonlit area, they were cut down by fire from the horsemen out in the darkness. They had their repeating rifles now and blasted into the running men, felling them all.

Turnbull crossed the open area in an instant, and moments later the raiders could be heard, over the moans of the wounded townsmen, galloping off into the darkness.

CHAPTER FIVE

It was close to noon when Doc Weatherbee arrived in Baker City. He had slept the previous night beneath his wagon at the side of the trail, but no one would have guessed this from looking at him. He was freshly shaved, perfectly barbered, his suit was unrumpled, and he sported a lime and burgundy silk vest which one grizzled freighter opined was bright enough to frighten off wolves. He left off his bags at Blind Danny's place and spent some time at the stables procuring Judith a comfortable stall. The stableboy saw no reason to treat a mule like a champion horse until Doc tipped him well.

Raider was nowhere about the hotel. As he had done, Doc took his time to observe what was going on before he identified himself as a Pinkerton operative to Daniel Brent. Brent looked him over, apparently none too pleased with what he saw—his motions were so natural, Doc forgot for a moment he was blind—then took him to a small office and closed the door after them.

"What the hell's going on here?" Brent snapped.

"Pardon me?" Doc inquired politely.

"First they send me out this big crazy man whose sole idea of investigation seems to be to shoot first and ask questions later. Next they send a city dandy who no doubt will charm the ladies and will get stomped on by the male population of this town. You behave like a sissy in this town, my friend, you won't last long."

Doc smiled. "Did your wife describe me to you?"

"Dang right."

"She said I was sissified?"

"I guess not." Brent paused. "Quite the opposite. She gave me such an admiring account of you, I figured you had to be a mother's boy. That's the kind women like."

"Not young pretty women, like your wife."

A flush of anger spread across Brent's cheeks. "She ain't that young! She's got a boy sixteen years old! You keep your hands off her! You'd be surprised to know how well I can shoot a gun."

"It wouldn't surprise me at all. I've seen the way you move around here. I guess you know every room. Yet I noticed how you reacted to unexpected things, like people coming your way. How do you do that?" Doc knew he was flattering the man rather than insulting him or bringing up an unpleasant subject. Brent forgot his disapproval of Doc while he explained how it was done.

"I can't see a durn thing, not if you set a mountain right in front of me. I feel things with my face. A lot of blind people can do this if they've been blind since they were very young or never could see at all, like I was. I hear that those who lose their sight later in life never learn to do it well. You could put me in a strange room, where I'd never been before, and I could walk straight at a wall and stop with my nose almost touching it but without ever actually having touched it. I can sense it's there."

"You ever make mistakes?"

Brent hooted with laughter. "The skin on my shins never heals. I'm always black and blue with bruises all over. But I never let that hold me back. If you want to live, you have to pay the price of admission. For some people, like me, for example, it may seem the price is higher than for others. Yet, in the long run, it evens out for everybody. Sooner or later we all have to pay some price, because the man who has something is the only one who can lose something. I got me a good wife and fine kids and a place I can call home. There ain't a large number of men in Baker County who've got what I have. I don't see myself as a deprived person or as someone deserving of pity."

"You won't be receiving any from me," Weatherbee told him.

"I ain't received none from your partner neither. Which is fine by me. Raider and I don't hit it off too well. He seems a difficult man to work with."

"He can be," Doc observed cautiously.

"I'm hoping us two see eye to eye," Brent went on. He described how he had been one of the first to campaign for Tom Turnbull in the election for mayor of Baker city two years previously. Turnbull had proved himself an excellent mayor, since he was, in Brent's opinion, the first man ever to hold that job who knew what he was doing. He had straightened out the town's finances, pushed necessary but unpopular votes through the city council, and completed things that had been left unfinished for years. Daniel Brent had always seen the potential of Baker City, and now there was a mayor who could realize that potential, make what was possible become real. Somewhere along the way, Brent had decided that what they could do for Baker City, they could do for Baker County, too. He supported the mayor's candidates for city council, built a new courthouse in Baker City, and acted as supervisor of the county elections. He couldn't say for sure when the mayor and his cronies had begun to show their hand. Once they were in power, they hadn't waited long. At first it was just small things. Then they started laying down the law according to their own private rules. It wasn't long after that before they started killing those who stood up to them. There were still some people in town who believed in the mayor. Not too many. And getting fewer every day.

Daniel Brent went on to say that the mayor and his cronies had staged a raid on Spirit Lake last night to obtain papers essential for county business that the town had been unwilling to hand over because of the supposedly fraudulent election. Although the raiders had kept their faces covered with bandannas, everyone knew who they were. The raider killed was a Baker City man charged with selling government rangeland to unwary land speculators. His partner in this had been the mayor. But no one could prove their identities.

"They'd have been big heroes in Baker City if it hadn't been for one of them using two girl children as a shield for the others," Brent said. "Nothing we like here as much as a good stylish raid. All the same, there's nothing we respect as much as womanhood. Now, that would've been a low and dirty thing to do with two grown women—even whores—but with two girl children it was way beneath what your average Oregon outlaw will stoop to. And I've known a few in my days on the goldfields. I wish those boys were here now. They'd plug the son of a bitch just for breathing the same air as them. Word's out it was the mayor who done it. Any supporters he still had in town, I reckon he's lost now. Neither of the girls was hurt, so some good came out of it. Though they had four Spirit Lake men killed and two wounded."

"Has Raider heard about it?" Doc asked immediately.

"Everyone in town is talking about it."

"I'm sorry to hear that you and Raider aren't hitting it off too well," Doc remarked.

"That Raider character is like having a grizzly bear on the premises. He rolls in and he rolls out, anyone who bothers him gets cracked on the jaw. No one in town has tangled seriously with him since he shot those four men, after I asked him to look out for a newspaper reporter fella who denounced the mayor. I think the mayor tried to hire him once or twice. I have to tell you I was kind of hoping for something different when you arrived. My son Cole warned me of what Raider was going to be like. He said you was the quiet and sensible sort."

"I am."

"That wasn't my wife's opinion."

Doc laughed.

"I'm sorry for my remarks about the way you look," Brent said. "I guess I was having a jealous turn. All the same, I was serious about shooting you if you so much as lay a finger on my woman."

"I'll keep that in mind," Doc said. Interested in techniques as always, he asked, "How will you do it? You rely on sound?"

"I ain't giving away none of my secrets, Weatherbee."

"I don't carry a gun."

"A blind man can't tell that, Weatherbee. Which makes it fair and square for him to shoot you."

• • •

When Cole Brent came into the ranch house, Joe Keefe hardly bothered to look up.

"Still scribbling?" Cole inquired.

"Damn right. I'm setting this all down—everything I've had to swallow and shut up about. Those I know most about are Fredericks and Turnbull, but I got a sprinkling of home truths about some of the others, too."

"My father, for instance?"

Keefe looked at him through his thick lenses. "Your pa made some mistakes of judgment in trusting the wrong men. He's not guilty of any wrongdoing. In these here articles of mine, I call him a blind old fool from time to time, but that's no more than I say to his face."

Cole sat on a bench and heaved his boots off. Keefe was already stooped over the pad of paper on the kitchen table again, writing quickly, crossing things out, muttering and cursing to himself, peering at the paper, his nose almost touching it.

"If ever I seen a man out to make himself blind, it's you," Cole observed.

"I never could see worth a shit. I got good ears, and that's where my stories come from. I probably walk into more walls than your pa. I guess I can see real good out to about nine inches, when I don't have my mind on something else."

"You ever read your newspaper?"

"I don't have time, young man," Keefe said briskly. "Now, if you don't mind, I have work to do. This piece needs some finishing touches and that'll be Fredericks and Turnbull nicely covered. I've not been wasting my days in idleness out here, young Brent. When these stories appear, no matter where they're printed, the county records will back up what I say and justice will be done. Mark my words on that."

Cole looked at him, surprised. "Of course you wouldn't have heard. I forgot to tell you. The mayor and some others raided the old courthouse in Spirit Lake last night. There was talk they had burned incriminating papers and evidence."

Joe Keefe went deathly pale and dropped his pen on the writing pad. He didn't bother to blot the splash of ink the nib spread across his lines. After a long spell of staring and mumbling, he said clearly, "I can prove nothing without that documentation."

Cole Brent had no idea what Keefe was talking about, and he had learned to leave the newspaperman alone in his weirder moments. He unbuckled his gunbelt, stood his Winchester in a corner, and went outside to gut a jackrabbit he had shot for their meal. When he came back in with the skinned, cleaned rabbit, he found Keefe's magnified eyes gazing uncertainly into his face as he stood trying to line up the barrel of Brent's shooting iron on his head.

"I won't be stopped," Keefe announced.

Brent would have laughed if he hadn't been afraid the revolver was going to discharge any second in this incompetent's hand. "Put the gun away, Joe," he said.

"I will not be stopped!"

"From what? You going to gun down the sheriff and the mayor outside some saloon in town, then ride for the hills?"

"I know you laugh at me, young Brent," Keefe said in a bitter voice. "Now step out of my way."

Cole moved obligingly aside and watched the puny newspaperman go out the door. He was a long time in the barn, hitching a horse to a wagon. When he drove past the house, Cole saw why. He had loaded the long guns stored there onto the back of the wagon, along with several crates of ammunition. Cole himself had brought those weapons and bullets from town yesterday as part of his efforts to fortify the ranch. He hadn't gotten around to bringing them inside the ranch house. Now this crazed scribbler was making off with them.

Cole had more guns inside the ranch house. He could easily have shot Joe Keefe off the wagon bench. Keefe probably hadn't thought about that. Best thing he could do, Cole decided, was saddle up a horse and trail along behind, giving Keefe his head so long as he stayed out of trouble. Cole could move in fast when something threatened and seize control of the situation.

With a sixteen-year-old's confidence in his own powers, Cole was not allowing for the fact that it might be too late by then for him to do that.

The Baker City *Sentinel-Advocate* had an interior loading bay to protect the newsprint from sun and dust or snow and mud. The horse-drawn wagons came in through a pair of big double doors on one side of the building and went out through a similar pair of doors on the other side after loading or unloading. Joe Keefe brought his horse and wagon inside at a gallop through the open doors.

Cole Brent had tried to cut him off as he had neared town. Keefe had fired at him as the youth attempted to reach out and grab the line at Keefe's horse's head. He had come closer to hitting him than he had intended, grazing Cole's mount in the neck with a .45 bullet. The cut horse took off like a bat out of hell, with Cole fighting to stay in the saddle. By the time he had quieted his bleeding horse, Keefe's wagon was at the edge of town. Keefe reached the newspaper building before Cole could catch up with him. Cole had the sense to see that things were now beyond his ability to control them. He would have to tell Raider he had let Keefe slip away from him. He headed for his father's hotel.

Meanwhile Keefe had stopped the wagon at the loading bay. No other wagons were there, and the freight handlers were taking a smoke and a rest. They were surprised to see Joe Keefe.

"Help me bring these rifles and boxes to the press room," he said.

They looked at one another and slowly got to their feet. They liked Joe. When he had been at the paper, he had never regarded himself as too important to stop by and talk with them, and he always included their births, marriages, and deaths as well as those of the rich folk in town. Joe Keefe had always done this on his own, and things had changed fast once he was gone, although it was only a short time. Neither Homer Fredericks nor the man he had found to replace Keefe wasted their valuable time on anyone at the loading bay. What the hell, if Joe Keefe wanted them to bring guns to the press room, that's what they'd do for him.

The typesetters and pressmen stopped work and stared when they saw the rifles and Keefe. He nodded to them casually and went around locking doors. The one-story building had several street entrances, and Keefe made sure all these doors, and those leading back to the loading bays, were secure before he let anyone know what was going on.

"I'm back on the job for this edition, boys," Keefe told them. "This week we'll only do one edition—same one circulates in the East as here. I've got four new lead stories. Kill your present leads and run these instead. Set them in type as fast as you can. We can still do the print run and ship on time this evening."

The typesetters took his copy, and the page makeup men unlocked their forms. Luck was with Keefe, because they had heard only that morning that Joe's replacement had been fired by Homer Fredericks. They naturally assumed Keefe and Fredericks had made some kind of truce to redo this issue. Only when the typesetters began their work did it occur to them that this was not the case. Nothing much was said until they ran proofs and the proofreaders went to work. They looked wonderingly at Joe and read choice paragraphs aloud.

All Keefe said was, "I don't want these stories cut. If they don't fit in the space assigned, kill some of the ads to make room."

The men worried about their jobs, but Keefe's prestige and their dislike for Fredericks kept them at work. The presses were running off the new revised edition of the *Sentinel-Advocate* after about three hours. No one had entered or left the building in that time. Things were going more smoothly than Joe had ever hoped. He couldn't take those stories anywhere else now that the evidence backing them had been destroyed. Fredericks could hardly sue his own newspaper for libel for printing the stories. But even with the newspapers coming off the presses, Keefe was far from confident. Publishing was the easy part, and would mean nothing without distribution. Fredericks could burn every copy of the edition unread if Keefe didn't get it shipped out and beyond Fredericks's control. Running the presses was still only the middle of the fight. He had to keep Fredericks from finding out what was going on until it was too late for the newspaper owner to do anything about stopping the edition.

Every man had more than enough to keep him busy as the press run progressed. The usual problems that occurred kept everyone too occupied solving them to ask any questions of Joe Keefe. Though nobody said anything, they had all noticed the locked doors. They might have jumped to conclusions about another man, but Joe Keefe was not easy to associate with rifles and crates of ammunition. The workers kept wondering and waiting to see who else was involved, and what they were involed in.

Cole Brent wandered past a few times. Once Keefe put his finger to his lips and Cole grinned back at him. Keefe guessed he had been unable to contact Raider, which Keefe regarded as another piece of luck. Raider was someone he would not care to have a disagreement with. He had no way of knowing that Raider had ridden out of town with Doc Weatherbee, to discuss him among other things. Cole Brent was just waiting for them to return, undecided what he himself should do in the meantime.

Keefe thought it might be Raider when he heard a heavy fist pounding on one of the doors from the loading bay.

"Tell him to go away," Keefe told the foreman.

The foreman did and was answered by a stream of curses and threats to break down the door.

"It's Hansen," the foreman said, something he didn't have to tell Keefe, who knew the sound of this voice all too well. Swede Hansen looked after things for Homer Fredericks, taking care of everything from a board that needed nailing to a head that needed cracking. Swede's idea of fun was to often bump into Keefe accidentally on purpose and send the smaller man sprawling.

Keefe picked up one of the repeater rifles he had loaded and levered a shell into the firing chamber. "Let him in."

"Joe . . ." the foreman protested.

"Before he breaks down the door," Keefe explained.

The foreman walked to the door and reached for the key in its lock. The printing presses were still chattering, but the flow of newspapers had slowed to a trickle as everyone watched. No one ran to seek cover, as they would have if two gunfighters had been involved. But Keefe was so shortsighted, he often couldn't find his pen on his desk, and Swede wouldn't need a gun because he would have no trouble tearing Joe apart with his bare hands.

The door was opened a sliver by the foreman and then flung all the way open by Hansen, who strode in. He had a bullet head with close-cropped fair hair on a neck so short it seemed to sit directly on his broad shoulders. His mouth dropped open when he saw Keefe. He headed for him with a roar, taking the rifle in the reporter's hands no more seriously than the others had.

Keefe saw a large, blurry shape charging him like a buffalo. He started shooting, levering a shell, shooting again, fast as he could, not pausing to see if any of his shots had connected.

"You got him, Joe! You got him! Quit firing before you kill us all!" It took several men to persuade Keefe to ease off with the rifle as he shot into the empty space in front of him, ricocheting bullets off the walls.

Hansen lay face down in a pool of blood, less than ten feet from Keefe. He had been too big for even Keefe to miss at that range. Joe just stood there, dazed, with gray smoke curling from the rifle barrel warm in his hand.

The foreman slammed shut the door to the loading bay and turned the key in the lock. "All right, you men, we can all see we're being kept here against our will at gunpoint, being forced to put out an edition by a man who has already killed and will not hesitate to kill again. We have no choice. The sound of the presses drowned out the noise of the shots. We're at his mercy. Back to work!"

He winked at Joe on the way back, but he was way outside the focal length of the reporter's lenses.

There wasn't much that could stump Judge Hayes. He always had a legal opinion ready for everything brought before him, and he never wasted time brooding about the fine points or gray areas of a decision. No sooner had he heard both sides than he might look up at the ceiling for a moment and then drop his decision on them. When he left the bench to retire to his chambers for a few moments, it was not to ponder in solitude but to take a few slugs from a bourbon bottle. Opinion was divided as to the level at which he worked best, some saying a pint, others going all the way up to a quart.

Today he was feeling cantankerous. So far those he had found in the wrong had been shown no mercy, and fortunately for them their cases had been minor, for the judge, when he was in this mood, was a hanging judge. Coleman Hayes had been on the bench for twenty years, all of them in remote areas where the gun was the only appeal to his decisions. His ways and methods would have shocked people back east, but struck many folks in Baker County as grass-roots and sensible. What people out in these parts did not want to hear was some old dodderer hemming and hawing about stuff no one could understand. They might not always agree with Judge Hayes, but they sure as hell understood and paid heed to what he said.

Sheriff Nate Cahoon didn't give a damn what kind of mood the judge was in. He had done his job well the previous day by taking these men out of Spirit Lake, and what went on today was only a formality as far as he was concerned. The judge could say what he liked; there was nothing he could do.

Judge Hayes ignored the Spirit Lake men brought before him on a whole list of spurious charges. Instead, he concentrated on the sheriff.

"Pity you weren't around later in the day, Sheriff, to stop those raiders at the old courthouse. Any idea who they might have been?"

"No, sir."

"Seems the papers they took ended right in this building. The ones that weren't burnt. But I don't suppose you know anything about that either."

The sheriff didn't. The judge harped on about the destroyed papers and mentioned the names of some of those who stood to benefit, including the mayor. He noted that the papers now in the Baker City courthouse included property deeds and mining claims. He warned that any case that came before him whose merits depended solely on these papers would receive special scrutiny for tampering with records or their deliberate destruction. The sheriff listened to twenty minutes of abuse from the judge, who then dismissed the case without ever saying a word to the defendants.

Raider and Doc Weatherbee looked in the Brent ranch house but could find no message.

"Keefe probably had a touch of cabin fever and Cole took him for a ride out on the range someplace or into the foothills," Raider decided. "I could take you around, except we'll be figured for Pinkertons soon enough if we go on a tour of inspection together."

"If I need to, I can take the wagon around and sell some medicine," Doc said. "You in a hurry to get back to town?"

"Reckon not. It wouldn't hurt to wait here awhile to see if they show up."

Keefe opened the doors to the loading bay when the freight wagons arrived at the appointed time to ship the weekly newspaper. Apart from the copies that went east, the *Sentinel-Advocate* was sold within the confines of Baker County, and most copies were sold within fifty miles of Baker City. Keefe knew that Homer Fredericks would quickly seize all the copies put up for sale in Baker City. He was relying on those that left the town. So he had the tied bundles destined for other places loaded first. Keeping out of sight himself, he had the foreman tell the Baker City deliverers to come back in a couple of hours because one press was down, causing the delay. There was nothing unusual about this, and the men went away grumbling. Sure now that the out-of-town shipments were gone too far to recall, Keefe allowed the Baker City papers to be turned over when they came back.

"I guess we'll be taking ourselves off now, Joe," the foreman said.

"You ain't going anywhere," Keefe said, threatening him with a rifle.

"We put out that issue for you. What more do you want from us?"

"I don't want anyone warning Fredericks or the mayor. Stay put. You can all leave later."

The printers and others were annoyed with Joe, but not enough to shoot him with one of the other guns. They could plainly see that Keefe was worked up enough to shoot any of *them* if they went against him. The foreman put them to cleaning up the presses and the floors. In a way, none of the men really wanted to leave in case they missed what was going to happen when Homer Fredericks looked at page one of the latest edition of his newspaper.

They didn't have long to wait. Fredericks came stalking down the main street. They could see him coming from one of the windows. He wasn't alone. Homer Fredericks was never alone, in spite of being a big man. He hired others to do his fighting for him when he could, although he was known to have gunned men down himself in fair fights.

"Keefe, the boss is on his way!" the men shouted. "He's looking mad as hell! He never thought he'd see your name as a byline in his paper again. He's going to fire us, Joe, but maybe he's going to kill you."

Keefe aimed his rifle out a window and loosed off three shots in the general direction of Fredericks and the men with him. He scattered them without hitting any of them. Two of them fired back from cover with revolvers, their bullets smacking harmlessly into the board side of the newspaper building. Others ran back the way they had come.

"They'll be returning," the foreman warned Keefe. "You'd better ride out while you still can."

"I'm stopping here," Keefe announced, loading cartridges into his rifle. "I brought along these extra guns in case any of you want to stay. The rest of you go."

"Joe, this is crazy! There ain't no point in having men killed over this. I say we all cut out right now. We'll hide you until it's safe for you to sneak out of town. You can ride north to Pendleton and make it to the Columbia River from there. Fredericks won't catch up with you."

"I ain't running," Keefe said. "I'm going to stand by what I wrote, no matter what. I let those bastards browbeat me and chase me out when I tried to have my say at the city council meeting. I've kept quiet for long enough—even helped them by doing all that fake news for the eastern edition. No more. I did wrong. I'm admitting it. Except now I'm going to make up for it and expose the ones behind it all. If I run off now, it'll look like I didn't have the courage of my convictions. It's my war, men, not yours. I appreciate what you've done today in getting that newspaper out. You had better leave now. This isn't your fight."

Some left fast, by the back doors. Others stayed for the moment, undecided and reluctant to abandon Keefe. The ones delaying were not doing so because of the fight against the corrupt mayor. They were hanging on for Joe Keefe and against Homer Fredericks. With Joe back for the day, they had been reminded forcibly of how things so recently had been better with him. They had thought they would never see the day when ads would be thrown out instead of cutting a story to fit the page. Now they felt guilty about walking out on him. But picking up guns and firing on Fredericks and his bunch was asking too much.

Keefe had no doubt about what he was doing. Resting his thick right lens almost against the rear sight of his rifle, Joe was blasting away at real or imagined enemies out on the street. One of Fredericks's men made the mistake of clowning around in the street, unafraid of the wild shooting from the newspaper building. The bullets were going every which way, and he didn't seem in any more danger of getting hit than anyone else. Yet Keefe managed to draw a bead on him and collapsed his antics with a single shot, leaving him lying on his back on the dusty street, clutching at his gut, with no help on the way.

Doc Weatherbee and Raider heard the shooting even before they saw the town. Cole Brent came out on foot to meet them. He told them about Keefe and swore that if he had ever dreamed things would have come to this, he'd have shot him in the leg back at the ranch to keep him there.

"Shooting a man in the leg isn't as safe as some folk believe," Doc said. "If you hit the main artery, he'll be just as dead as if you'd hit him in the heart. If you break a bone, he may lose the leg or die fairly easily from a number of things. You're just going to have to mark this one up to experience, Cole."

"At least I kept the marshal out of it," Cole said. "The sheriff left town before this started, so that's one good thing. The newspaper owner and about a dozen of his hired guns have laid siege to the newspaper office. There's a lot of shooting on both sides, as you can hear."

"The marshal's letting this go on?" Weatherbee questioned. "Let's go see him. Not as Pinkertons. As friends of Joe Keefe."

Marshal Earl Sloane already knew Raider well because of the four men of Fredericks's that he'd killed while protecting Keefe. He hadn't listened to Fredericks's demands that Raider be held for murder then, and he wasn't too surprised to see Raider coming on the scene now. An old gunslinger from the Kansas cowtowns, there wasn't much that ever surprised Sloane. He walked with a bit of a limp where his leg bones hadn't knitted properly after a fall from a horse. His mustache was gray, but his eyes and movements were lively and keen. Not too many men had wanted to try their luck against Earl Sloane in Baker City, and none of those had succeeded.

He greeted Raider warily. "Young Brent here will have told you what's goin' on, I guess. Seems Joe Keefe took crazy and ran his own version of the *Sentinel-Advocate,* forcing the men at the plant to work at gunpoint. That's what the ones told me who escaped. Keefe is still holding many of them prisoner inside, and he fired without warning on Fredericks and some men as they walked down the street. There are witnesses to that. One of the printers claimed Keefe had shot Swede Hansen dead inside the plant. Look at this week's newspaper for yourself. I can't hold Fredericks back from trying to regain possession of his property."

Weatherbee was all set to argue, but Raider held his hand in front of his face. "Sloane," he said, "you and me is going to clear the street *and* the inside of that building. First we start with the street. Are you ready?"

The marshal shrugged. "I have some men—"

"You don't need them," Raider told him. "You just tell them to stop shooting, and if they don't do what you say, I'll shoot them."

"Just like that?" the marshal asked with a grin.

"Just like that."

The two men walked down the street, with Cole and Doc close behind them. They were exposed to fire from both sides as they neared the building but did not draw any. One man lay dead in an alley. An onlooker told them that several more of Fredericks's men had been injured and taken to the doctor. Their side had been reinforced by the men who worked for the mayor, and they kept up a steady fusillade of rifle fire at the windows of the newspaper building. Their fire was returned sporadically. Often there was no fire until one of Fredericks's men showed himself and then a few accurately aimed bullets made him lay low again.

"We'll nail the bastards when it gets dark, Marshal," one gunman said. "They'll never be able to stop us coming in close then. If it weren't for Mr. Fredericks's belongings, we could've burned the place over them by now."

"And maybe the town as well," Marshal Sloane said dryly. "Don't load that rifle. You're doing no more shooting in my town."

The man obeyed him and hung back to see what would happen. Two more shooters who saw him obey the marshal did the same. The next man along wasn't having any of it.

"I do what Mr. Fredericks and the mayor say, not what some run-down old fella who should be in a rocking chair—"

Raider cut in. "You do what the marshal says or you show me how mean and fast you are, boy."

Raider had laid it on heavy, and there was no way for the shooter to save face now. He had to bow down or else throw lead.

He swiveled his rifle barrel toward the big Pinkerton and tried for a fast hip shot. He was quick, only the long barrel of the Pinkerton's .44 revolver was quicker. So too were the thumb that snapped the hammer and the finger that pulled the trigger. Raider placed the bullet between the man's eyes, and he crashed down as a life-less deadweight.

"Mr. Fredericks," the marshal called, "I'm asking you to go home next."

Raider smiled as if the notion of doing the same thing to Homer Fredericks would cause him happiness.

Fredericks backed down with a lot of complaints and demands for justice. His men and those of the mayor went with him.

The newspaper building was silent. The two Pinkertons, the marshal, and Cole Brent approached it deliberately. When they came to a door, they heard it being unlocked from the inside. It swung open for them. The marshal went in first, followed by the others.

"He's over there," a printer directed them.

Joe Keefe was in a sitting position against one wall, a bullet in his left forehead.

Raider bent over him, lifting off his spectacles, which still hung from one ear. He touched the man's cheek. "He's nearly cold. This man has been dead for hours."

"They got him early," the foreman said. "It was us who done all the rest of the shooting. For Joe's sake."

"I didn't hear that," Marshal Sloane growled. "Next time I look around, I don't expect to see none of you here."

Cole Brent stooped alongside Raider over Keefe's body. Tears ran down his cheeks. "I'm sorry, Joe," he sobbed. "I should've stopped you."

"No way," Raider said. "Joe Keefe was set on re-deeming himself for what he fancied he had done wrong. Cole, you shouldn't stop a man from doing that, and doing it his way. We all got a right to do that."

CHAPTER SIX

There was a big turnout for Joe Keefe's funeral. Judge Hayes showed. And the marshal. Conspicuously absent were the mayor and Keefe's ex-boss, Homer Fredericks. The sheriff was out of town. Sheriff Cahoon spent most of his time out of town on the mayor's orders, because Mayor Turnbull wanted to avoid conflict with the marshal and judge as much as possible. A man of Cahoon's temperament was not the kind to coexist easily with enemies, and for that matter neither were Judge Hayes or Marshal Sloane. The mayor stayed home. So did Homer Fredericks. Their men killed in the siege of the newspaper building, including Swede Hansen, were buried with only their gravediggers as mourners. The diggers dropped their pine boxes into the earth and rattled stones and soil in on top of them with no delay. A big crowd was gathered for Keefe's send-off. No clergyman being available, the judge read a long passage from the Bible about the children of Israel in the land of Moab, for no particular reason that anyone could figure out.

Everyone at the Star Saloon afterward remembered something funny or touching about Joe Keefe. Many praised his courage, without actually mentioning the things he had said about the mayor, Fredericks, the sheriff, and some others in his final article for the *Sentinel-Advocate*. Everybody in town who could read had read the latest edition, and those who couldn't had it read aloud to them. In days that edition, maybe for the first time, would make its way to the state capitol of Salem and to cities like Portland and Eugene. In a week, it would be on Wall Street in New York City, and in Washington, D.C., and in less time than that it would have found its way to members of the stock exchange in San Francisco. Tom Turnbull was finished as mayor of Baker City, they were sure of that, and maybe Nate Cahoon as sheriff of Baker County, which might be hard to arrange because of the countywide status of his vote. But for the moment, both those gents still held power, and while they did there were few who wanted to tangle with them by bringing up anything as unpleasant as those newspaper articles. Joe Keefe hadn't survived to boast of writing them. Joe himself must have known he wouldn't. Anyone could have told him that. As with all brave men, there were more willing to drink to his memory than take what he had to say to heart.

Weatherbee and Raider kept well back, part and yet not part of the crowd. They didn't talk with one another, trying to keep their identities as Pinkertons from becoming known. Doc intended to bring out his wagonload of medicines that afternoon and drum up a few sales to keep his reputation as a traveling physician intact.

Daniel Brent left to attend a city council meeting at noon. Gradually the crowd broke into those who had work to do elsewhere and those who were going to drink the day away. Some games of chance got started. However, Valerie saw nothing to interest her at any of the faro games. She came over to talk with Raider.

As soon as Doc saw him talking with the pretty

woman, he started drifting over their way. When Raider saw him coming, he grew flustered, remembering how many women he had lost to the smooth-tongued Easterner. Raider could never figure out what women saw in Weatherbee. It was enough for him to know that Doc attracted them like flies to dung.

"You want to move on someplace else?" Raider asked Valerie.

"I just got here, Raider. What's eating you all of a sudden?"

"Nothing."

She could see that there was. She hadn't handled being a woman and a professional gambler this far west without being a keen observer. Valerie was good at spotting things before they happened, which allowed her time to step sideways if need be. She noticed Doc headed their way. "That sharp dresser an acquaintance of yours?" she asked.

"Who?" Raider pretended not to see.

"Handsome fella with the gray derby."

"I seen him around town," Raider conceded. He scowled in Weatherbee's direction, which of course only encouraged Doc.

Sweeping his derby off his head, Doc bowed to Valerie and then turned to Raider. "Is this your younger sister, whom you've told me so much about?"

"I ain't told you nothing about any sister," Raider rasped.

"He won't admit it," Doc said to Valerie. "But I can see the family likeness. You are his sister, aren't you?"

Valerie smiled and said, "You're full of shit."

"Weatherbee is the name. Traveling physician. I guarantee to cure what ails you."

"I'm sure you do," Valerie said tolerantly. She told

him her first name and her profession. "Now if you want to try your skill in faro, I'd be mighty pleased to sit with you."

"Faro," Doc said doubtfully. "I don't believe so."

Doc was not used to this treatment from a woman, but he wouldn't give Raider the satisfaction of showing his surprise. He again tipped his hat to the lady, wished Raider a pleasant day, and moved on.

Raider was so flabbergasted at seeing Weatherbee receive the cold shoulder from a woman—treatment he himself was accustomed to getting—that he could think of nothing to say to her.

Valerie mused, "Pity to let him go, really. He was so handsome and polite. I kind of liked him."

Raider found words fast. "He's a louse!"

Valerie laughed. She leaned across and kissed Raider full on the mouth. She said, "I like my men the way I like my whiskey—raw and rough."

Raider said nothing, only grinned. He was feeling like some hardscrabble miner who has just uncovered himself a hunk of gold.

Nate Cahoon rode with two men northward along the Powder River Valley. Here and there they had seen land cleared close to the river by farmers who planted crops instead of herding cattle or sheep. The labor involved in clearing roots and rocks from the soil in order to make it suitable for planting kept most men away from this type of activity. Besides, it was only along the stream edges and valley bottoms that the land was rich enough to support farming. So it was said. And everybody believed it except Dr. Kringer and his followers at New Hammelburg.

The sheriff and his two men rode another half hour

before they saw the huge area of the Powder River Valley cleared by Kringer's old-country Germans. The two men had never seen the fields with ruler-straight rows of vegetables and the groves of trees near large frame houses, an island of regularity, maybe three miles by four, in the tangled wilderness all around.

"These here must be Mormons, like you have around Salt Lake City," one man said.

"No, these ones speak German with each other," Cahoon told him. "They're Christians, like you and me, except they believe in brotherly love and sharing what they've got with one another. That don't mean they're generous enough to pay the county the extra taxes we want from them." He laughed.

"It's sure impressive what they've done here. I ain't never seen nothing like it afore. We going into the town, sheriff?"

"Kringer himself warned me off last time I was here. Crusty old bastard. All his followers up and run when he tells them to do something, so he's used to being obeyed. But he can't tell the goddamn county sheriff to keep off, and I aim to show him that in a friendly way. That's why I brought you two boys along. I don't want no killings done. Only a little reminding he don't talk to me like I'm some kind of nothing horse thief drifting by."

"This Kringer sure got himself some spread here," one of the men said admiringly.

Cahoon taunted him, "Maybe you want to start living peaceful and clean, working hard and saying your prayers."

The man took him seriously. "I remember when I was like that, back in Ohio. It ain't so long ago neither. But it seems way, way back. I was better off then than I am now or ever will be again, only I was fool enough not to know it. Naw, Sheriff, it's too late for me to ever go back to what I was. But I don't grudge an admiring word for them who never wandered from the straight and narrow."

Cahoon looked at him with a sneer. "I'd send you back to Baker City right now, 'cept I know you for the coyote you are."

The town of New Hammelburg was in the center of the cultivated area, three streets of two- and three-story frame houses. Each house had a tall brick chimney at each end. Men in the streets wore old-fashioned black suits and women wore dresses and bonnets, just like in old pictures. The children were dressed and behaved like miniature adults. There were stores, but no saloons, gaming halls, or brothels. No one looked at them directly, not even the children, as they rode their horses slowly along the street. Yet all three men were acutely aware their every movement was being closely observed.

"You get the feeling there's people looking down gun barrels at us from inside those houses?" one of the men asked.

"There are," the sheriff said shortly.

They dismounted outside one large three-story house with a two-deck porch across its east front. Four men emerged and came forward to meet them.

"Dr. Kringer home?" the sheriff asked.

"Not to you, Sheriff," one man said. "But I can tell you we've paid all our legal taxes, and to assess us for any more, you'll have to go before Judge Hayes."

"And you've talked with him, I bet," the sheriff said sourly. "Well, what I'm here about today is the taxes due on places of entertainment in this town."

"We don't have places of entertainment in New Hammelburg," the man said stiffly.

"If you had," the sheriff said, "they'd have to assume the burden of most of your taxes."

"This is a God-fearing, law-abiding, hardworking community, and we'll have no whores, gaming tables, or hellish red-eye in our town."

Cahoon ignored him and pointed to an orchard of black walnut trees at one end of the town. "Some Baker City investors is interested in buying up that land and opening up this town. They'd take care of most of the taxes and bring a lot of extra business here. Right now, folks stay away because this place is duller than a prairie dog town."

"We don't exclude outsiders from living here or having a business here, Sheriff. They're welcome. We don't demand that they attend our churches. Before they come, though, they should know that this is a dry town and that no public sinfulness is permitted. We aim to keep it that way. None of your Baker City saloon owners will be allowed to open here. Nor will we sell land to any of them."

Cahoon nodded patiently. This fella was one of Kringer's sons, who had been born at the community's original settlement in Missouri and had legal training back east. He spoke English with a German accent, like all the others, in spite of being born in America; yet even if he sounded funny, he knew his lawbooks. Cahoon had warned Turnbull, Fredericks, and the others about these younger ones who could effectively take over if they got rid of old Kringer. In Cahoon's opinion, it was these young ones who needed to be got rid of. Cahoon himself was part owner of three Baker City saloons, and the mayor and Fredericks each had ten times his stakes in entertainment establishments. The sheriff knew that the remarks of Kringer's son were aimed at him personally. But he was going to be patient.

"Listen to me good and careful," he said, pointing his forefinger into the other man's face. "This town has gotta have progress, and the people who want to bring it here ain't going to be stopped with words or with some fool laws a drunk judge thinks up. Tell me how you think you're going to keep these men out of here."

Kringer's son looked distressed. "We'll resort to violence in self-defense. For instance, if you were to go for your revolver right now, Sheriff, at least four rifle bullets would hit you before your gun had cleared its holster."

That was the kind of thing Cahoon had been waiting for. "I'm going to take you in for threatening a county peace officer. Get your horse. You're riding into town along with us."

"No, Sheriff, I'm not. I'll send a written protest to Judge Hayes tomorrow. I doubt he'll accept your charges."

"I wouldn't bet on that old moonshine judge being around to pester us much longer," Cahoon said evenly. "But I'm tired of jawing with you. I just came to tell you that you no longer have any choice about selling that land for a fair price and opening up this town. Maybe when that deal goes through, I'll try to forget about the threatening you done against me today."

He nodded to his two men, wheeled his horse about, and led them at a slow walk out of town.

The mayor of Baker City sat at the head of the long table in the conference room in the courthouse basement. The city councillors sat along the sides of the table, with Daniel Brent in the last chair on one side. Homer Fredericks sat in the second-to-last chair on the opposite side. Apart from the mayor's place, there was no pecking order in regard to chairs, those arriving usually occupying the nearest empty chair.

The mayor was saying, "I want to put it to a vote that this council denounces and despises the pirated edition of the *Sentinel-Advocate* which carries those libelous and maliciously untrue stories about certain prominent citizens in this town. It will mean something to outsiders if this resolution is passed unanimously. All those in favor raise their hands." The mayor raised his own hand, as did four of the seven councillors. "All those against?" Daniel Brent alone raised his hand.

The mayor smiled. "I see we have two nonvoters and one blind man who couldn't read for himself the item in question. It was probably misread to him by one of the malcontents who seem so eager to give Baker City a bad name. So, gentlemen, we have a unanimous vote from the voting councillors condemning this edition, including the newspaper owner himself."

Daniel Brent shouted, "Mr. Mayor, I protest—"

"Next order of business!" Turnbull shouted him down. "We are pressed for time, gentlemen. We must move along."

"Sorry to keep you boys waiting," Tom Turnbull told the two men sitting on a corral rail at the livery stables. "I had a town meeting to attend, and as usual there were a few contrary folk intent on giving me a hard time. I'm too easy on them, and I allow them to waste my time."

They saddled up and rode a ways outside of town before they talked serious business.

Turnbull said, "The gold in the veins is spotty.

Shoots are short. But there's parallel quartz veins all through the rock, and these veins persist. So it's a lot of labor, with a guaranteed return. This mine has been a steady earner for two years now, and it's hardly been properly worked, with one old-timer picking at it on the days he feels up to working."

"If it's like you say it is, Turnbull, we got ourselves a deal," one of the men said. "But me and my partner here ain't the sort to be pushed around, so be careful what you promise us. We intend to hold you to it."

"We go three ways on everything," Turnbull said. "One share to each of you, and one to me. All the gold goes to the assay office here in Baker City. What you get is a working gold mine with no purchase price and no expenses. What I get in exchange for finding you this will be one-third of the assayed value of the gold. This arrangement lasts until the lode is worked out or until the mine is sold, when I get one-third of the selling price. I don't see any room for misunderstanding in that."

"You'll get your third all right if you give us what you say. A man don't get a present of a working gold mine every day of the week."

"This ain't a present," Turnbull said deliberately. "It's a change of ownership and a new working relationship. No one is giving away anything for nothing."

The two men nodded.

One asked, "You brung along the papers?"

"We'll look at them when we reach the top of the ridge," the mayor said.

They climbed the steep trail up the side of the ridge, winding among pine trees. Near the summit, the trail ran alongside a deep gorge. They could look down on the tops of tall pines growing at the base of the gorge.

The mayor pulled his horse to a stop. His horse stamped on the rocky ground and jerked its head. "Easy, boy. He's nervous because he smells wolves. There's more wolves up here than deerflies, and you can see there's plenty of them." He dismounted and tied his horse to a tree trunk. "Old Maloney never fails to come this way to town every day. He likes to have a few drinks in town late in the afternoon and head back to his mine well before sundown. When you boys are out this way, you're going to have the same problem making your way along here before it gets too dark."

"We've lived in worse places," one of the two said gruffly.

"Here are the papers." Turnbull showed them the bill of sale, signed with Maloney's faked signature, which stated that he had sold the mine to them the previous day for two thousand dollars, payable in gold within forty-eight hours. "My man at the courthouse remembers him being there with you two, and all the papers are in order there. Here's the signed receipt for the two thousand, dated today. And here are all the duplicate papers to the claim in case you can't find the originals. When you get out to the mine, burn all his belongings, especially any papers or letters. I know he has no will filed and almost certainly has no known next of kin. So we should have no troubles. You paid him his money and he rode out of here without saying where he was going. Men do it every day."

The old miner showed right on time, riding his burro along the trail toward town. Turnbull drew his rifle from its saddle sheath. He hit the miner in the center of the chest with his first shot, knocking him off the burro's back and down into the gorge. He brought the burro to its knees with a shot to its forequarters and finished it off with a point-blank bullet between its eyes. All three had to push the heavy carcass over the side.

The mayor looked down into the gorge. "No sign of them from here. The wolves will soon scatter their bones, and the buzzards will pick them clean." He looked coldly at the two men. "Time you two went out to that mine and got busy with your picks and blasting powder."

They mounted up and rode on. The mayor stood awhile before riding back to town. Occasionally he liked to be alone in wild country like this. It gave a man time to think.

Doc Weatherbee hadn't had much luck selling his cures and medicines around Baker City, but then he hadn't been trying very hard. He spent much of the time talking with people he met along the way. None of them had a good word for Sheriff Cahoon, who seemed to spend his entire time collecting taxes all over the county. No one knew what became of the money he had been successful in collecting. Certainly the county had nothing to show for it. The other big beef among most of them was that Tom Turnbull, elected as an official only to Baker City, was really the boss of the whole of Baker County. In other words, Doc heard nothing he didn't already know, except for a fresh bunch of incidents involving money-gouging and land-grabbing on the part of the sheriff. Although no occurrence was big enough in itself to cause major excitement, Weatherbee realized that the large number of these happenings indicated the size of the fortune the sheriff and his cronies were stashing away. Weatherbee also guessed that with control of the county records, they could now disguise a variety of land sales for their private enrichment.

Daniel Brent had imagined that they had only wanted to seize control of Baker City and had achieved their goal. Weatherbee now saw that he and Raider had not come in at the end, but only at the beginning. These men were not looking for power and glory in small-town politics. They were making a clean sweep of the whole county's funds. Things were now just getting under way for them.

Keefe's newspaper articles would alert state and federal authorities to what was going on, though it would take a long while for them to make their influence felt in this lonesome stretch. In the meantime, it was up to Raider and Doc to make things uncomfortable for those who hoped for a smooth ride.

Back in Baker City, he returned Judith and the wagon to the stables and sauntered over to the nearest saloon. Doc's mouth nearly fell open when he saw the stunning beauty sitting alone at a table inside. Up till now, Raider's girl, Valerie, had been the prettiest in town, and she had taken a dislike to him, much to Raider's relief. But what he saw now blew Valerie clean out of his mind.

She wore her ash-blonde hair piled up under an extravagant hat, and the pale blue silk of her gown revealed the curves of the voluptuous body inside. She gave Doc a frankly curious stare.

"This is no country for a doctor, ma'am," he said to her, raising his derby. "Everyone hereabouts is strong as a horse and healthy as an elk. You look a picture of health yourself."

"I get a stitch in my side when I run."

A concerned look came over Doc's face. "Which side?" he asked.

Although Doc had been correct in guessing there was

not much wrong with her, she did need a sympathetic ear for her complaints. Doc supplied sympathy and understanding. She told him she was an actress with a theater troupe about to appear in town and remarked how fortunate she felt to have met such a perfect gentleman in these unlikely surroundings. He gallantly told her of his even greater amazement to meet someone as beautiful and cultured as she. She would be delighted to have dinner with him. They had fun over the meal, which turned out to be salmon, as usual. Doc was already getting to feel that if he didn't see salmon on his plate for another ten years, he wouldn't object. Aurora —she admitted that this was her stage name and wouldn't tell him her real name because it was "too ordinary"—accepted his offer of a drink in his hotel room. She too was staying at Blind Danny's place, although she referred to it as the Majestic.

In his room, they talked some more over a few glasses of bourbon. When she removed the silk wrap around her shoulders, Doc thought nothing of it. When she continued to slowly and deliberately disrobe, he could not hide the smile of anticipation that spread across his face. His eyes drank in the beauty of her body as it was slowly revealed to him. Naked, she lay on the bed and writhed in suggestive poses.

Doc knew he was meant to watch, not touch. This was one theatrical lady who liked to put on a show. Finally she beckoned to him to come between her parted legs. He dropped his pants fast and pulled off the rest of his clothes. He knelt between her thighs.

She took his swollen cock in her hand and eased its knob inside her. Doc pushed deep into her, and her hips began to move in a slow rhythm that teased his cock as he pumped it into her.

His thrusts grew more urgent and her rhythm wilder as their bodies slapped against each other in a fierce struggle of possession. She cried out and bit into his shoulder to quench her scream as she climaxed violently. Successive convulsions ran through her body, then died away, only to begin again. At length she lay sobbing beneath him. But Doc wasn't finished yet.

He shifted his weight off her onto his elbows and began to kiss her gently as she lay quietly beneath him. His cock's head lay just inside the placid lips of her sex as he slowly excited her body and roused her passions again. He heard her breathing grow faster and felt her tremble.

He started to thrust softly and slowly into her, and her moist receptiveness welcomed him. He brought her to orgasm once again. This time he exploded a stream of sperm into her, and his body spasmed in intense pleasure as he delivered the fruits of his manhood deep within her.

CHAPTER SEVEN

Nate Cahoon was still burning at the way he had been treated in New Hammelburg. Kringer's son had stood up to him and lived to boast about it. A sheriff wouldn't last long in a place like Baker County if that kind of story made the rounds about him. Here a lawman was expected to be faster and meaner than everyone else— otherwise what was he? Nate had to send a message back to Kringer and he had to send it fast, before anyone started to get wrong ideas that it was all right to stand up to him and threaten him.

He had spent the night at Spirit Lake, just to show the inhabitants of that town he was going to continue to be part of their lives. Anyone who wanted to try to change the course of things had his chance to do so. No one took him on.

Next morning he and his two men saddled up. They had expected Cahoon to ride south from the town, to collect money from the sheepherders with flocks out that way. Instead, he headed back the way they had come the previous day, toward New Hammelburg. The two men looked at each other and said nothing. Cahoon was doing a slow burn, and neither man wanted the sheriff's rage to spill out on him by saying something to annoy him.

Cahoon spoke when he was ready to. "Trouble in dealing with them community people is they got everything they need in their own town and don't ride anywhere else except on special occasion. So you don't catch none of them alone and far from home. When Kringer sends them someplace, he sends a bunch together, well armed. Same thing when you ride into their town. They watch you like you were a grizzly that wandered down off the mountains. I could get a band of men together and we could have a big shoot-out. That'd make me feel better—to lay a crowd of them bastards under the sod—but word would spread about what happened, and in the end it would do them more good than me. What I want them to know is that they're gonna have to open up that town to outside investors and that they can't talk to me like I'm some nickel-and-dime marshal of a fleabag town."

They rode on in silence for a while, not driving their horses but setting an easy pace, the way men do when they're not certain about their next move.

Finally one of the men said, "I see some of the community men alone. I see 'em all the time."

Cahoon looked at him, startled. "Where?"

"At work in their fields."

A look of understanding crossed Cahoon's face. "I never thought of that," he admitted. "They were right in front of my nose and I didn't see them. Dang, that's where we'll go. To their fields."

Men were saving hay in some fields and weeding waist-high lines of corn in others. Some cleared irrigation channels. The three riders kept well distant, on a trail through thorn scrub that hid them most of the time.

They saw a lone man working on a wooden sluice gate in an irrigation channel; he wasn't far from the others, but he was out of their sight because of a sheltering row of trees planted alongside the channel. Cahoon removed his star and all three pulled their bandannas over their faces as they rode toward him. They covered him with their revolvers when they came within a few yards of him.

He was in his late twenties and unarmed except for a hammer and nails. He looked up at them fearlessly. "I carry no money," he said. "None of us brothers do. If you are hungry, ride into town and you will be fed just by asking. If you want work, we will give you that for a fair rate of pay. You do not need to draw your gun or hide your face in New Hammelburg. We will not abandon any man of goodwill."

"Shut up," Cahoon told him. "We don't want your charity." Cahoon holstered his gun, and while the other two kept the farmer covered the sheriff bound his wrists behind his back with a rawhide thong. "Put your guns away," he said. "The sound of a shot will bring the rest running."

The community member took his cue from that and began yelling for help. A short chop to his gut from Cahoon left him too breathless to make any sound louder than a croak.

The sheriff examined the sluice gate under repair. It was a square made of boards, about three feet by three, which could be raised or lowered in two slots, like a guillotine blade. When it was lowered, it blocked the main water channel and backed up the water into side channels across the field. Raised, it allowed the flow onward, which was less than two feet deep. Cahoon shut the gate down again and let the water back up.

"Bring him here," he told the two men.

Following Cahoon's instructions, they forced the struggling farmer face down in the channel on the empty side of the gate. While Cahoon slowly raised the gate, the two men forced the farmer's head, against the flow of water, into the gap beneath it. When the man's chin was past the baseboard, Cahoon dropped the gate on his neck and held him pinioned beneath it. The two men released their hold and let him thrash.

Cahoon kept pressing down on the gate, and the three men looked down at the jerking head of the drowning man on the deep side of the gate. A half foot of water gurgled beneath the gate, and the farmer's legs splashed in this as he kicked, managed to get to his knees, and tried unsuccessfully, his hands tied behind his back, to jerk his head from beneath the gate.

His body flopped full length again, and his kicks and splashes grew weaker as his body could not draw oxygen from his water-filled lungs and he gradually lost consciousness.

The sheriff waited a few minutes to make sure he was a goner. "Old Kringer is smart enough to get the message from this." He smiled. "Specially when it occurs to him that the only place he can come for help is to me."

Daniel Brent stalked up and down Weatherbee's hotel room, turning about only inches before he crashed into the walls. Earlier he had tried stalking up and down Raider's room, but it hadn't worked out because of Raider's belongings strewn around the floor, which caused him to continually trip.

"Neither of you is worth a damn," Brent was saying. "Every time I look for one of you, you have a bottle, a playing card, or a woman in your hands. I didn't bring you two out here to have a good time. I brought you here to clean up this town. If anything, all you've done is add to the lowlife activities since you've arrived."

Raider snorted and called him a silly old fart.

Weatherbee lit an Old Virginia cheroot and blew a thoughtful cloud of smoke in the air, which set Raider to coughing and hacking and cursing some more.

"We hadn't known, Mr. Brent, that we were to be moral guardians of this town," Doc said coolly. "I'm sure you didn't have your son mention that role to Mr. Pinkerton. If your son had, he would have been turned down."

"I expected simple, clean living agents—"

"Mr. Pinkerton prefers to have his employees in the field known as operatives," Doc corrected him in his coldest, politest voice.

Raider shook his head at this, beginning to feel sorry for the blind man because of the nasty way Weatherbee was treating him.

"I don't mind you so much, Weatherbee," Brent growled. "Half the time you behave like a human. It's you, Raider, that gets to me—behaving like a goddamn animal all the time."

"I was feeling sorry for you," Raider said, genuinely hurt at Brent's attack on him. "Weatherbee's right. You *are* a contrary old cuss and we *are* going to have to step on you if we're to have any peace."

"I could just as easy pack you both back where you came from," Brent shouted.

"And have your ass shot off within a week when word got around that we were Pinkertons," Raider told him.

"You wouldn't leak that information?" Brent asked.

"I don't believe that Pinkertons would stoop to such a low trick."

"You said yourself we weren't regular clean-living Pinkertons," Raider answered, winking at Doc. "I wouldn't leak that information, but I think Weatherbee would."

"It would depend on the circumstances," Doc added solemnly.

Brent was shouting again, running through his fairly limited vocabulary of obscene insults. A hardworking family man like Brent is often hard put to find the exact word to display the intensity of his rage.

When he was through, Weatherbee yawned and said, "Danny, by your own admission you've been suckered in for months by what was going on in this town. For us to clean up the place, you've got to at least give us a day for every week you spent messing it up."

"Wastrels!" Brent shouted. He strode to the door, opened it, walked out, and slammed it behind him.

"Not bad for a blind man," Doc said admiringly.

"You think he really is?" Raider wondered.

From the ranch house window, Cole Brent saw the horseman approaching. He drew a bead on him with his rifle and waited. He lowered the rifle when he recognized Henry Barlow, who had been to school with him in Baker City although he was from New Hammelburg. All the older boys went to school in Baker City for their last few years because the school was by far the best in the whole of the eastern part of the state, even if it was in the jaws of hell, so far as the community members were concerned. Although it was frowned on for community members to make free with outsiders, there were no set rules against it. For some time Henry Barlow had been riding off quietly to meet Cole Brent. They talked about going east for further education, which both their fathers wanted them to do, while their mothers wanted them to stay home. Cole had more or less decided against going, liking his work on the ranch. Henry changed his mind from day to day.

Cole's sudden trip to Chicago aroused Henry's curiosity. He didn't buy the story that Cole had gone to check out an eastern school, and bit by bit he dragged the information from Cole that he had gone to hire "professional gunmen" for his father. Cole would say no more and did not reveal they were Pinkertons. Henry wondered why he had to go all the way to Chicago for gunfighters when he could have found a couple in most of the saloons in town, but he had to be satisfied with Cole's story because he could pry no more information out of him. Then Henry met Joe Keefe while he was staying at the ranch house, and heard what happened at the newspaper building. Now he was visiting the ranch almost every day. They didn't have exciting stuff like that in New Hammelburg. At last not until today, they didn't.

Henry could barely wait to unsaddle and water his horse before telling Cole the news. "They found my cousin stuck under an irrigation gate this morning a while after people noticed the sheriff passing by. They're sure Cahoon done it, because he was out threatening us yesterday and he was run off our land."

They discussed all the morbid details of the man's drowning. Henry described the widow's screaming and the dead man's boy being too young to understand what had happened, saying, "I know he's drowned, but when is he coming home to play with me?"

"Makes me damn riled when I hear of some harmless

man like that getting killed by them who don't deserve to live," Cole said angrily.

"We believe repentance can save any man from his sins," Henry said sincerely.

"What?" Cole laughed derisively. "Even Nate Cahoon?"

"Even him."

"You're full of crap," Cole said.

"It's harder to believe with some than with others," Henry granted. "But although we believe it's not too late for him to repent, we're taking precautions in the full expectation that he won't."

"None of you is any good for fighting. You know that."

Henry looked a bit ashamed. "I wouldn't tolerate no one but you saying that, Cole. I'd whup any man that'd dare make a statement like that in my presence."

They both cracked up at the idea of that.

"But seriously, Cole," Henry went on, "remember those professional gunmen you went to Chicago for? That fella Raider who killed those men in town—he's one of them, isn't he? I seen him a couple of times, and he looks a mighty dangerous character."

Cole grinned. "I ain't saying Raider is, and I ain't saying that he's not."

"You said you were getting two. Who's the other one?"

"You seen a fella in a gray derby and wearing a fancy suit like he was going to his wedding?"

"The traveling doctor fella?"

"That's him," Cole announced. "Weatherbee."

"He don't look like no gunfighter to me," Henry said with certainty.

"That's the way they are in Chicago," Cole said. "I

didn't think too much of him either when I saw him first. I was thinking of sending him back until I heard."

"Heard what?"

"Heard about how Weatherbee does his killing," Cole said.

"Come on, tell me. How does he do it?"

Cole's eyes narrowed and he lowered his voice. "Straight razor. He slips up behind a man sitting on a bar stool, draws the blade across his throat in an instant, then, *splat!* the fella's artery empties itself on the mirror behind the bar and he drops dead in the sawdust without a drop in his veins."

Henry thought this over and looked impressed.

Cole was enjoying himself. "Follows people home too and creeps in the window while they're asleep." He drew his finger across his throat. "Does it so gently, they never even wake up."

"You think him and Raider would help my community against Cahoon?" Henry asked.

"I don't know what my father would say. I hear he's being difficult."

"So don't tell him."

That sounded like a reasonable suggestion to Cole.

A bit past ten that night, Raider was taking it easy in the Egyptian Palace while Valerie played high-stakes faro with some flush miners in a hurry to get rid of their gold so they could hardscrabble in the hills again. Raider and she had an agreement whereby *he* never pressured her to quit playing until she was good and ready to do so, and *she* made it worth his while waiting, after they left together.

Despite Daniel Brent's opinion of him, Raider had been on his best behavior now for days on end. He had cut back his liquor intake drastically, and he'd backed off from more than a dozen fights. Even he himself knew it was all too good to last. The first cloud on the horizon was the mayor of Baker City. Tom Turnbull arrived alone and settled himself next to Raider.

"You ain't found a job yet?" he inquired.

"I ain't done a lot of looking," Raider drawled.

"There's some who say you're in the pay of Jason Wymes."

"There are? What am I supposed to be doing for him?"

"That's what I was wondering," the mayor said. "Jason and me don't get along too good. He's been keeping his nose out of my business lately, and I hope things stay that way. Now, if you are working for him, I don't see why you should be staying in my town all this time, instead of out on his grazing lands. What use has he for you in town?"

"You'd have to ask him that."

"I'm asking you," Turnbull said sharply.

"I hate to see a busy man like you waste his valuable time," Raider said with a friendly smile.

Turnbull decided not to get mad. Instead, he became confidential. "Look, we can talk with each other. I know you must have a generous arrangement with Wymes. A man like you deserves one. Let me improve on it. You come to work for me and I'll double whatever Wymes is giving you. I'll pay in gold and I'll accept your word for what your present pay is. You can't beat that."

"I'll think about it," Raider said amiably.

"Like hell you will. I want your decision now. Yes or no."

"A man like me don't take to being rushed into things."

"Yes or no," the mayor repeated.

Raider laughed. "Try me some other time."

Turnbull's face grew rigid with anger. "How long more do you hope to stay in this town?"

"Haven't thought about it," Raider said vaguely.

Turnbull stood. "You better start thinking about it and make up your mind before I reach that door."

"Good night," Raider called after him.

Valerie was doing well at the faro. The miners weren't, but they weren't letting this hold them back from having a good time, and all of them were making a lot of noise. The men drank, and Valerie would have to pay a percentage of her winnings to the saloon owner, so everyone was happy. Raider was aware that the man who had just left was part owner of the saloon. The sheriff was another. That was how things often worked in a town this size.

The mayor was going to make a move against him, Raider was sure of that. They would see who was boss in this town. What the mayor didn't know was that this was the kind of move Raider had been waiting for him to make. The Pinkerton guessed he would find himself suddenly unwelcome in most of the saloons in town. Raider had to admit this would be a deadly blow against him. He was kind of relieved when two gunfighters he knew to be in Turnbull's pay walked in after a little while and worked hard at pretending not to see him. If this was all the mayor had in mind to keep him in line, Raider felt he could handle it easy.

"You boys come in here looking for me?" Raider called down the bar to them.

The gunfighters glanced at each other, startled by this move and not liking it much. They said nothing and studied their drinks.

Raider figured they were both in their early twenties, almost kids, that they were fast, but that was all, not too bright, not as experienced as their easy swagger was supposed to suggest. Young, mean, fast—that could be a deadly combination. It usually was. Two against one was a great help also. Yet Raider had surprise on his side. He had already thrown them off balance, and he knew they wouldn't strike against him until they felt sure of their ground. All he had to do was keep a few moves ahead of them. Talking was not going to do it with this pair.

"I can see that the mayor didn't send two skinny, jumpy fellas like you to beat on me with their fists and boots," Raider said in a loud voice to them.

The miners had quieted at their faro game, as had most everyone in the saloon, except for a few who were too far gone to notice anything short of a major earthquake.

The two gunfighters still did not react, other than by refusing to look in Raider's direction. Raider was sure of himself now—this was not the way two men would behave who happened to be in the mayor's pay yet had only come in at this time by coincidence. These shooters had been sent to gun him down, and things were not going the way they had expected them to, and they weren't sure what to do at this moment.

They stiffened when, out of the corner of their eye, they saw Raider leave the bar and circle around behind them. Being back-shooters themselves, they were naturally inclined to think this was Raider's intention.

Gamblers were scooping their money off the tables

and moving fast out of what they considered might be the line of fire. Things had gone very quiet, except for the occasional chair overturned in someone's hurry.

Raider had eased his gun out of its holster by now, cocked it, and held its barrel down close to his right leg, so he couldn't be said to be threatening anyone with it.

"You better put your shooting irons on the bar in front of you," he said to the mayor's men. "The barkeep will hold them for you till you leave."

He was maybe fifteen feet directly behind them now. If they wanted to draw and fire on him, they had to make a quarter turn to do it. And there was no way they could go on ignoring him. Very, very soon they either had to throw lead at him or docilely place their weapons in front of them for the barkeep to confiscate. If there had been betting on the outcome—and there wasn't—the odds would have been high against a peaceful resolution. Raider wasn't providing them with an out so they could back away with their pride intact. The way Raider played it, there could only be winner and loser, no matter how things were settled. It was plain which Raider expected it to be.

One of the men muttered something to the other, glancing back over his shoulder. The other nodded. They both slowly pulled their revolvers from their holsters and made as if to lay them on the bar. However, instead of placing them flat on the counter, they both whipped around, snapping back the hammers of their .45s as they came.

Raider jerked up the long barrel of his .44 Remington and shot from the hip. Flame spat from the muzzle as the bullet sped on its way, caught the gunman on Raider's right in the lower gut, traveled through his intestines, and shattered his pelvis.

The Pinkerton snapped back the hammer with his thumb as he raised his weapon to chest level and knocked off his second shot. This bullet caught the other gunfighter square in the chest and knocked him back on his ass at the base of the bar. He died without getting off a shot and with a surprised look on his face that remained there after life had gone.

CHAPTER EIGHT

Henry Barlow sat in with the community's Council of
Guardians when they met the next morning. It was not
forbidden for him to do so, yet his appearance there
indicated that he had something important to say. His
father, a regular member of the council, seemed to find
it hard to believe that his son was sitting there without a
word to him beforehand. When it came to open discus-
sion, everyone looked at young Henry expectantly. He
raised his hand and received a nod from Dr. Kringer,
who sat at the head of the long table.

Henry spoke politely in the German dialect used at
the settlement. He glossed over certain things. He didn't
say bluntly that New Hammelburg men were not much
use at fighting. He didn't tell them how Weatherbee
killed sleeping people with a straight razor. And he
didn't mention that he made regular trips to talk with
Cole Brent, instead making it sound as if they had just
chanced to meet. He did mention Raider and Weatherbee's names and said they were hired by Daniel Brent to
clean up the mess in Baker City. Since it was known to
all that Sheriff Cahoon was part of the mayor's gang,
these two hired gunmen should be willing to confront
Cahoon any chance they got. If Cahoon was going to

harass settlement people, then the community should invite them out and give them the run of the place.

A few men, whose reactions were always predictable, rose to denounce Henry for dealing with "outsiders" and wanting to bring sinful desperadoes to New Hammelburg.

Henry's father stood and looked sternly down the table at his son. He said, "It always comes as a bit of a shock to a father to find his son becoming a man in his own right. Whether you gentlemen agree or disagree with his suggestions, I think my son's motive in dealing with people outside our community is clear. As every one of us must, he is standing up for our way of life and seeking ways to protect us from our enemies. This time the threat to us is coming from outside our community. I think we should consider carefully whether, as Henry suggests, we need help also from the outside." He sat down to a general murmur of assent.

Dr. Kringer's face was an impassive mask. As usual, no one could guess which side he would come down on. He believed in letting everyone who wanted to have their say before he made his decision. When the decision was made, everyone had to obey it.

"I never thought I'd see the day when we would hire assassins to murder and pillage on our behalf," one man said earnestly. To back up what he said, he told them the news he had heard from Baker City—that only last night this gunman named Raider had killed two of the mayor's hired guns in the Egyptian Palace saloon.

This report worked against the man's argument rather than for it, since all it did was back up Henry's contention that here were two deadly killers way too vicious and crazy for even Cahoon and Turnbull to handle.

Others had their say. Apart from the ones who

wanted no contact with the outside world under any circumstances, there seemed a guarded willingness to go along with Henry's suggestion. Dr. Kringer did not keep them on tenterhooks for his decision.

"First of all, let me join with Henry's father in his support of his son. I think the young man is a credit to this community. As you know, his father was not from the old country and married into our group when we were in Missouri. Many were not pleased when that event took place. They have been proved wrong. I do not think that our faith and principles are so weak that we cannot risk any contact with those who do not think and live as we do. We must only be aware of the risks of doing so. The presence of these two gunfighters would present a risk to our community, but their presence would help counteract the even greater risk presented by Cahoon and his associates. I think it would be wrong for us to *hire* these men, but we are not being asked to do so. Daniel Brent has already done that. It would be foolhardy of us not to make use of them on our own terms. Henry, invite them to talk with us."

Henry Barlow rose at the end of the meeting no longer regarded as an empty-headed youth but respected by the others as a man they would have to contend with.

The glory days of the Oregon gold rush, starting with the discovery of gold in Griffin's Gulch in the fall of 1861, were now past. There were still many rich miners and many rich mines—which these days tended to be lode veins that had to be chipped from rock rather than the comparatively easy digging of gravel in placer deposits in streambeds. As the gold played out, the mining camps folded one by one as the miners moved on to fields with richer strikes. New strikes and new fortunes were still being made, but these were now uncommon occurrences, instead of being the almost daily news they had been more than fifteen years previously. The great days of sudden fabulous wealth lived on only in the eastern edition of the *Sentinel-Advocate* and in the minds of some unwary Wall Street speculators.

Chinese workers, released from construction crews on completion of the transcontinental railroads, poured into the region to pan the tailings of abandoned mines. Barred from naturalization as citizens and from owning land, they had to be satisfied with the leavings of others. Besides panning cast-off low-grade ore, they washed old bins, chutes, mortar boxes, and amalgamating plates and blanketing for gold that might have collected in them. They searched behind old mill liners, in launders and elevator boots. They looked in spillage on floors. They burned wood and cloth and smelted the ash. They ground scrapings and sweepings with mercury and retorted the mixture. For this they were fiercely resented by many, as if there were some crime in taking what no one else wanted.

They were harassed, robbed, and sometimes murdered by bands of "stalwarts." Away from railroad work crews, the legal status of many was uncertain, and so was their grasp of the English language. Only a few could make their complaints understood, but that hardly mattered, because there was no authority for them to complain to. For the stalwarts, it was open season on Chinamen.

Jason Wymes couldn't bear the sight of them. He knew that his wife employed one to wash the family clothes and that she had hired another to work in the kitchen of their home in Baker City. His clothes were clean and the food served at home was good, so he kept his mouth shut. Besides which, his wife had a mind of her own and would not tolerate his meddling in her domestic realm. She could easily make things uncomfortable for him if he interfered, and Jason, with a solid middle-age spread, was fond of his comforts.

His best men were culling his herds, preparing for a cattle drive east. Few of them were willing to undertake the weeks of constant riding—often with only a few hours' sleep—and the thirst, boredom, and hardship of a long drive. Experienced hands could earn the same money by staying put on a ranch. The attraction of the Wymes spread was that it was within riding distance of Baker City, so the cowhands there could work from sunup to sundown and drink, gamble, and whore from sundown to sunup, so long as they had money. A cowhand's pay rarely exceeded forty dollars a month, so they spent more nights at the ranch bunkhouse than they did in Baker City—but at least they knew Baker City was there within reach, even if they couldn't afford it. Most ranches were a two- or three-day ride from the nearest town, and cowhands got to visit them once a month. Which accounted for why they acted so crazy when they did hit town. In Baker City, a quart of whiskey cost $1.50, and brandy or gin $1.25. The only man to own a toothbrush paid fifty cents for it.

Because most of his steady, experienced men would leave his employ rather than go on a cattle drive, Jason Wymes had been putting together a crew of whatever he could find. Now his problem was to keep them occupied and amused, so they wouldn't drift off on him before the cattle were ready. Most were no good for ranch work, and his regular men spurned working with them. That was when Jason thought of taking them with him to roust some Chinamen.

Chinese working the abandoned mine tailings were welcome in Baker City, where storekeepers specially stocked rice, ginger, tea, and all kinds of preserved and dried fish for them. Wymes had been irked by their presence on tailings in foothills bordering on the range-lands where he grazed his cattle. They hadn't interfered with his animals, and they hadn't trespassed on his lands. In fact, both the Chinese and his beeves were on public lands. Wymes just didn't like the idea of their being there, but he hadn't had the time to do anything about it until now. Running the Chinamen off the foot-hills would be something to do for the men he had col-lected for the drive, and it would amuse them.

He led the ones sober enough to ride to the nearest tailing, a big spill of earth and broken rock down the side of a hill beneath a tunnel, as if some giant rodent had gone to ground there and kicked out tons of earth with its rear legs. Four Chinese men with pigtails, dressed in loose blue clothes, panned soil from the tail-ings in a tiny stream nearby.

Wymes had seven men with him. They brought their horses to a canter on a stretch of level ground, then climbed them up the hill slope faster than the Chinese could run. The men beat the Chinese over the head and shoulders with lengths of timber they had brought along for this purpose. Everyone got a chance to get some blows in before all four of the Chinese lay bloodied and unconscious on the ground.

Some of the men tried to get their horses to step with their steel-shod hooves and place their weight on the prone bodies, but all the horses refused to do it, even when whipped and spurred.

Wymes laughed. "You critters are more low-down than the animals you ride. Don't waste your time. We got more of these Chinamen on the far side of the next hill."

Cole Brent opened the ranch house door and walked out with his rifle ready to shoot from the hip.

The Chinese man in front of the others kept bowing to him and saying, "Duibuqi." Then he said clearly the English words "Jason Wymes," pointed to the bruises and clotted blood on his head, and said, "Ta bei wo dale."

Cole lowered his gun and beckoned them inside. He had no idea what the man's lingo meant, but he knew Jason Wymes and he knew the signs of a beating when he saw them.

The four Chinese on their feet carried in the three they had slung across two burros. One was dead. Cole boiled water and fetched medicines and bandages. He let them mess with a couple of frying pans and his supplies at the stove to work up their own concoctions. He reckoned they would all be fine in a day or two, except the dead one, who needed to be put in the ground soon on account of the heat. The one not hurt bad helped him dig a hole, and the three others who could walk came out with food offerings to spirits, Cole guessed, after they laid the body in the hole. What interested Cole was that they seemed to be genuinely upset at the man's death, just like regular people.

He went back with them inside the house and ate some of their weird food, which tasted as weird as it looked. Cole had eaten worse and even had a second helping after he opened a brandy bottle and passed it around. He rarely drank himself but had heard that brandy had medicinal value. The Chinese certainly seemed to think so. One of the men who had been barely able to move sat up after a couple of swigs from the bottle held to his mouth.

Cole was sitting at the kitchen table, feeling most peculiar after several slugs of the cheap, fiery liquor. Even though he was a little dizzy and nauseous, he remembered to keep a wary eye out. He had got into the habit of this now. While indoors during the day, he peered out windows all the time and scanned the open land on every side of the ranch house. At night he stiffened at the slightest sound or woke from his sleep at even the rustle of a breeze in the long grass, like Indian braves are said to do.

Out the window, he saw horsemen approaching. He tried to count them, but each time his blurry vision played tricks on him and he got confused beyond the count of five. There were somewhere between seven and nine of them. He grabbed his repeating rifle and levered a shell into the chamber as he ran out the door.

The men saw him and kept coming. They were near enough now for him to recognize their leader. It was Jason Wymes. Cole became aware of the two burros tied to a hitching rail in front of the house. He had forgotten to set them loose in one of the corrals. Cole assumed Wymes must have known whose they were, and that now he was coming to finish off the unfortunate Chinese. Cole raised his rifle to his right shoulder, found the front sight bead in the rear sight notch, and placed it square in the middle of Jason's fat face, raising and lowering the barrel in time with his movements in the saddle.

Damn, his vision had been blurry before, and he had felt sick and dizzy. Now his belly muscles were knotted hard with determined rage, beads of sweat trickled down his forehead and dropped off his eyebrows, he could see clear for miles like an eagle, his hands were rock steady, his forefinger curled over the trigger. . . .

Cole had been practicing shooting an hour a day and had got so he could hit almost anything within three or four shots. But he knew that practice shooting was one thing and the real thing was another. A lot of expert target shooters were no good in a fight because they crumbled under the strain. Cole didn't feel like crumbling. Damn, he felt good!

Wymes still rode at him in spite of the rifle raised to his shoulder. Probably thought he could face down a chickenshit kid with his hard-man tactics. Showing off to the men riding with him. Cole would show him.

He looked down the sights at Jason's small eyes set wide apart and his fat cheeks. His barrel kept raising up and down with the man's motion in the saddle. His finger tightened on the trigger. He raised the bead to Jason's hatband and squeezed home the trigger.

The hat flew off Jason's head and landed in the grass behind him. Wymes reined in his horse and dismounted. He walked over and put his hat back on his head. He shook his fist once at Cole, remounted, and rode away, followed by his smirking men.

Whether he is a ranch hand or a big landowner, there's nothing a cattleman hates as much as being made to look ridiculous. Being thrown from a horse, bit by a rattler, or hit by a bullet could happen to any man, and his name would be none the worse for it. Being stood off by a kid with a rifle who blew your hat away and chased you from his land makes you the butt of a funny story. It made Jason Wymes mad just to think about the half-useless men he had hired for his cattle drive making fun of him in Baker City saloons. A public apology would help. He'd make Blind Danny bring his son into town to say he was sorry. Then he could either boot the kid in the ass or appear understanding and forgiving, depending on his mood and how young Brent behaved himself.

Daniel Brent was sitting in the lounge area off the hotel lobby, smoking his pipe and talking with Raider and Doc Weatherbee. Wymes joined them and complained about Brent's son, taking his hat off and poking his finger through to holes in front and back of the crown.

"He mustn't have recognized you," Brent commented.

"Course he knew me. That fool boy of yours knows me to see since he could walk."

"Then you must be leaving out part of the story, Jason," Brent opined. "As it stands, it don't make no sense."

Wymes snorted and added the facts about the Chinese Cole Brent was sheltering from him, as if this were an unimportant afterthought.

"I'm proud of my boy," Brent announced. "He'd be within his rights if he had put that bullet through your forehead, Wymes, instead of through your hat."

Jason Wymes looked genuinely astonished that Brent could feel this way. "You siding with them Chinamen against one of your own kind, Danny?"

"I brought Cole up to extend a helping hand to any man that needed and deserved it," Brent said quietly. "When I first came up to these parts from Kentucky, there were some who picked on me because they thought I was weak. There were others who gave me a helping hand precisely because they saw they were stronger than me. I been talking all these years about it to my kids, and I see that where Cole's concerned I sure haven't been wasting my time. I told you, Wymes, and I'll say it again—I'm proud of the boy."

His temper getting the better of him, Jason said. "I got a good mind to put a bunch of my men together and take a ride out to that ranch house and show—"

Raider, who along with Doc had kept out of things until now, put in his say. "You better watch your backs while you're riding out that way, Mr. Wymes. I'm going to be following real close behind you. Or maybe I'll be waiting for you out along."

"Now, take it easy, big fella," Jason told Raider, an uneasy smile on his face. "Danny and me is old friends, and we like to kid each other along. I don't want you taking serious anything I said. Danny and me is the only ones left in Baker City, along with the judge and marshal, who are willing and able to stand up to Turnbull and Cahoon. He and me are friends. So don't go developing misunderstandings about me. Look, if it upsets you all for me to chase some Chinamen now and then, I'll quit doing it. Why? Because I value you as friends. And, Danny, you can tell that wild kid of yours he doesn't have to buy me a new hat. At least living out there in the ranch house with them Chinamen, he'll have clean clothes to wear. Ha, ha. But don't you go standing up for sheepherders, Raider. I draw the line with them coyotes. There ain't room in Oregon for them."

Aurora's play opened that night in Baker City. Unlike many of the big mining towns, Baker City did not have a proper theater or concert hall. The play, named *The Willow Copse*, was staged in a poorly lighted warehouse, where the flickering kerosene lamps threatened to set fire to the wooden walls. Since there were no adequate changing rooms for the players, the actors and actresses had to walk from their hotel room along the street in full stage costume and makeup. They were cheered as they walked along and probably were responsible for selling out any tickets that yet remained. The house was full.

The crowds were brought out by the fact that there was not much to do in Baker City that didn't involve a bottle, a woman of easy virtue, or cards or dice. Anything out of the ordinary brought people flocking. They even came out of doors to watch the stagecoach arrive. It was not this alone that brought them to the play. The cast included not one but two famous actors—the immortal Couldock and the celebrated Jack Langrish.

Weatherbee had seen both men perform in New York City. There the theaters had been filled with glittering lights and splendid scenery, and the audience had consisted of elegant ladies and polite gentlemen. Weatherbee was intrigued to see how Couldock's magical voice could hold this rough Baker City audience spellbound in a warehouse with almost nonexistent scenery and awful lighting. The great actor raved and ranted, he sobbed, he laughed maniacally and waved his arms, he stamped his feet on the boards, he whispered, rolled his eyes, hissed words, stared silently. . . . The audience dared not move. Everyone forgot they were only watching a play, becoming so involved with what was taking place.

Aurora didn't have a big part. Like the other actors, she didn't have the presence and power of Couldock and Langrish and, as a result, was swamped by them. But she did her best and obviously enjoyed every minute of it. Doc, Raider, Valerie, and Daniel Brent saw to it she got a big hand. They were not alone—quite a section of the audience showed their noisy appreciation of her good looks. The play was a big hit, and there was talk that it might run three weeks or even a month in Baker City. This was fine by Doc. While the play lasted, Aurora stayed.

Neither he nor Raider were feeling pressured by Daniel Brent's complaints about the lack of quick results. Brent knew what they were up against better than anyone. There was nothing they could do until Turnbull or Cahoon stepped out of line far enough to give them just cause to act. If the judge and the town marshal had been different sorts, things might be easier. But Judge Hayes was ornery when drunk, ornerier when sober, and regarded his having had to move to the new Brent-financed courthouse as the full amount of outside interference he was willing to tolerate. Marshal Sloane, on the other hand, was helpful, but not in the way Doc Weatherbee wanted—like Raider, Sloane saw justice coming out of the muzzle of a gun. If Aurora's play lasted a full month, Doc guessed he might still be here, assuming nothing happened to him. That was the way a man in the field had to work—wait with patience for the right moment to strike. While he waited, Doc saw no reason not to enjoy himself as much as he could.

After the performance, Doc walked Aurora back to her hotel room so she could change out of her costume and stage makeup. As they went down the street, she glided her hand inside his coat, partly unbuttoned his vest, and slid her fingers inside his shirt.

"No wonder actresses have a bad name," Doc told her, smiling.

"I don't think I can wait until we reach the hotel. What would they do if we took off all our clothes and did it right here in the street?"

"Throw a bucket of cold water over us," he said.

"I guess you're right," she said. "I'll try to hold out till we reach the hotel."

They climbed quickly up the flight of stairs to her room, and Doc turned the key in her door. Once inside, he reached his arms around her shapely body as she threw herself passionately against him. He pressed his mouth on hers and ran his fingers over the curves of her body. She responded to his touches and peeled her clothes off to bare more of her flesh for his attentions.

They never got as far as the bed. She stretched out, trembling and quivering, naked to his gentle strokes, on a thick rug by the window. Doc shucked off his clothes and lay down beside her. He ran his fingers and then his tongue over her entire body. She sighed and twisted, presenting herself to him and shuddering with desire.

She eased herself beneath him and pulled him on top of her. He slipped his cock into her. As he drove it deep inside her, she moaned with pleasure.

CHAPTER NINE

"There ain't nothing anyone can do about it except send in the Army," Tom Turnbull said, "and the federal government ain't going to do that on the say-so of a state governor—especially not one of a western state. Hell, if the government sent the Army everyplace a scheming politician wanted them to, the soldiers would be spread thin all over. The Army ain't going to make a move in Oregon again unless it has to. These last few years, they've had more than enough from Chief Joseph and the Nez Percé, and the Bannocks and Shoshones. There ain't nothing the governor can do about us out here, and there ain't nothing the federal government is willing to do about us."

"I still say them newspaper stories by that rat Keefe done us all a lot of harm," Nate Cahoon replied.

The sheriff and mayor were riding slightly ahead and out of earshot of six men.

"I know you been hearing stories, Nate," Turnbull said. "I know they been saying my days as mayor are numbered, that folk in Baker City are going to run me out of town. That's only the kind of talk that weak men use to work up their courage. They're trying to persuade themselves and each other that they have the balls to do something about it. They don't. They're like rats—only time they're going to bite back is when they're cornered and can't run. So we'll ease up on them and they'll calm down right away."

"We can't ease up on them," the sheriff said. "We need money to pay our men. I ain't using *my* money to do it. That's put aside. And I don't see you giving back any of that gold you took. But we better have money for them next week, or there's no saying which side they'll be shooting on if we don't."

"Kringer and his crowd are rotten with cash. Them Bible thumpers don't spend it on nothing anyhow. All they do is work and pray. What do they need money for? It's only right they should pay a little more taxes than folk with expensive bad habits."

Nate laughed at this. "You ain't going to be easy to root out, Turnbull, I'll grant you that. But even if no one comes after us from outside Baker County, no one's going to send us help either if we run into trouble. Them newspaper stories have left us with no friends."

"All the more reason we should stick together, Nate. Ain't nobody strong enough to take us two on. Homer Fredericks is gonna run a long series contradicting what Keefe wrote. Time will heal that. People forget fast when you give them other things to think about."

"Kringer ain't gonna let us into his town."

"He ain't gonna be able to keep us out," the mayor said. "When they come over first from Germany, they was a few years someplace back east and then moved on to Bethel in Missouri. In the twelve years they spent there, they farmed six thousand acres and built homes, mills, and stores. Then old Kringer decides there's too many godless folk around them and heads out here to

Oregon. So they done even better here. But my point is this. They've gone just about as far west as they can go, unless they want to move on to China, and Kringer is an old man now. He wants to sit back and look at the fruit of his labors, not pack the community's belongings aboard wagons and head into the wilderness once again. The other older men will feel the same way. They'll strike a deal with us real fast just as soon as they see they have no other choice, but not before."

Cahoon said nothing. He had been against riding out so soon after he had drowned the farmer in the irrigation ditch. But Turnbull was adamant, wanting to keep the pressure on them. Since Turnbull was the brains of the operation while he was the brawn, Cahoon went along with what the mayor wanted.

When they neared the river valley settlement of cleared land with the town of New Hammelburg at its center, Cahoon asked, "How does it go?"

"What you did seems best," Turnbull answered. "Hit them where they're weakest. Out working in the fields."

Cahoon nodded and turned in his saddle to beckon the six men to ride closer behind them.

They made no effort to conceal themselves this time. The sheriff hid his star, and all of them pulled their bandannas up over their noses. They rode fast in a tight pack along the edges of the fields, ignoring individuals and pairs at work until they came to a small group of ten or so.

"Right, boys, these'll do!" Cahoon yelled and spurred his horse.

The farmers looked up as they saw the horsemen coming. They shouted and scattered toward a line of trees.

"Hit them before they reach cover," Cahoon shouted, figuring the farmers might have rifles stashed among the trees.

They all opened fire with their rifles on the running men, and knocked down four of them before they reached the trees.

"Let's go!" Cahoon called. "Move smartly now. We're in the open and they have the cover. You're asking for a bullet in your back."

The men moved quickly, although no shots followed them. However, Turnbull's horse mired down in soft ground recently flooded from a ditch. The animal twisted its back as it panicked trying to free its legs from the mud. Turnbull was thrown. He landed face down on the soft mud and was unhurt. The horse, though, had damaged its hindquarters and now, free of the mud, was unable to walk.

"Pull your bandanna up!" Cahoon shouted as he returned to Turnbull's aid. "You and you," he called to two of the men, "put down that horse and bring along the saddle and bridle. Tom, you jump on behind me. This colt is strong enough to carry us both. We're in luck them dumb farmers ain't got rifles."

"You can bet they will tomorrow," Turnbull said with a grim smile.

Many of the storekeepers and barkeeps came outside their places of business to stare at the men from New Hammelburg. It wasn't often that any were seen in Baker City above school age. Now, all of a sudden, here were fifty of them, riding like a cavalry company down the street, toting old-fashioned needle guns and huge, ancient scatterguns fit for a museum. They halted outside the courthouse and remained in their saddles, looking neither to right nor left. Maybe half a dozen of them dismounted and went inside the courthouse.

Judge Hayes was on the bench, trying not to doze off as he listened to an interminable wrangle over water rights. He had already made up his mind on the case and was only listening to all this twaddle, before delivering his verdict, for legal appearances. As soon as the six Kringer community members came in his court and his clerk whispered in his ear that there were many more outside, the judge looked interested, gave his verdict, and brought his gavel down on that case.

The spokesman for the farmers described to the judge how all six of them had been in the fields with four others and been attacked by masked riders. Two of the farmers had been killed instantly by rifle fire, and two had been wounded, one badly. The judge had already heard about the drowning, and he was looking fiercer and fiercer by the minute as he listened to this tale. Marshal Sloane came in at this stage, and the judge had the farmer describe the event over for him. Then the farmer made a statement that just about poleaxed the judge and marshal, who were both getting ready to explain why they could do nothing to help. All six of the community members in the courtroom had recognized Mayor Tom Turnbull as one of their attackers when his bandanna fell from his face. They had no doubts and readily swore on the Bible to it.

The judge immediately issued a warrant for the mayor's arrest on a charge of murder. He seemed to be almost in a good humor.

The marshal wasn't so taken by how things were working out. "Those killings weren't done in my town. That ain't my responsibility."

"Marshal, this warrant is good from Portland to Philadelphia," the judge thundered. "That ought to make it valid also in Baker City."

"I'll take him in," the marshal muttered.

"We'll stay in town to help you," one of the community members offered. "We—"

"You lot go home," the marshal said with a scowl. "You came here asking for help, so you'll get it. I'll take care of Turnbull my own way. If you want to deal with him yourselves, be my guest, but do it outside my town."

"We want a proper court trial," one of the farmers said.

"Go home," the marshal said wearily. "We'll let you know the date."

As the marshal headed for the exit, Judge Hayes called after him, "Sloane, I want Turnbull taken alive."

The court clerk thought he heard the judge add in a low voice, "So I can hang him."

It was nothing new for Earl Sloane to watch the hours slowly pass and listen to the ticking of the clock on the wall as he waited for a wanted man to show. He had done it in he had forgotten how many little cowtowns in Kansas as a marshal or deputy. Sometimes the wanted man never showed; sometimes he showed when least expected. Baker City was no different from any of those places down in Kansas. Word of what was happening had spread quickly, and now everyone in town was waiting along with him, looking at the nearest clock from time to time or fishing out a brass watch by its chain from a vest pocket, lifting its cover for a moment, then putting the watch back with a sigh. Folk passing the marshal's office looked in with a smile. They seemed mostly to be happy at the prospect of losing their mayor.

Sloane had been around too long to believe it would go that easy. Turnbull was not just another gunslinger or desperado. There was money riding on Turnbull, and his supporters were not going to let him sink without some effort to help out. Homer Fredericks and Turnbull's other cronies in town would hire him the best available lawyer, from Portland maybe, which might drag on the case, and meantime they would try to rouse sympathy for Turnbull in town, which would be no easy task for them. The mayor had ruled by fear, and his friends were powerful but few.

The marshal was more concerned about Sheriff Cahoon than about Fredericks and the others. The judge had countywide powers, but so did the sheriff. The sheriff could make things rough for him, as he undoubtedly would do. As marshal, Sloane did not answer to the sheriff, but a man whose power is limited to a town can't easily take on the whole county.

Earl Sloane sat at his desk in the marshal's office and listened to the clock ticking on the wall as he waited. The cells were empty. Three deputies were playing cards among themselves, and Sloane could tell their hearts weren't in the game by the lackluster way they played. They too were watching and listening for something else.

Finally word came. Tom Turnbull had arrived in town. Right now he was in the Star Saloon and had heard about the warrant for his arrest. The man who'd brought the news said that the mayor claimed he'd been with the sheriff all day, looking over some land they were thinking of buying together. The sheriff had gone back to Spirit Lake, and Turnbull had sent a man to bring him to Baker City as quickly as possible.

Marshal Sloane didn't have to be told he had to act before Cahoon got into town. Apparently Turnbull expected to hold him off until then, or else the mayor knew he couldn't run out of his own town to hide until the sheriff arrived and then come back and expect to take over again. Sloane would soon find what Turnbull had in mind when he went to the Star Saloon.

"Let's go, men," he said to the three deputies, whose card game had already broken up.

They walked warily in the door of the Star and peered about them in the gloom. Turnbull stood at one end of the bar. It seemed to Sloane that half the men in the place were on the mayor's, sheriff's or Homer Fredericks's payrolls. The three deputies had plainly reached the same conclusion and were showing no signs of any great wish for a fight. Hanging back, they waited to see how the marshal would handle the situation.

"Stay by the door," he told them and walked alone across the saloon to where Turnbull stood at the bar.

Turnbull stood ready to draw, backed by his men, right until the marshal stood at the bar next to him.

"You heard about that paper the judge signed," Sloane said to Turnbull. It was a statement of fact, not a question. He went on, "Don't seem right to arrest a mayor in his own town. How about you and me walking by ourselves back to my office to discuss our problem?"

The mayor thought about it for a moment. "Sounds good to me. Have a drink on me before we go?"

"Sure."

All eyes followed the two men as they left the saloon together, the mayor waving the marshal through the door in front of him and Sloane presenting his back to the man he was taking in as he went ahead. They said nothing to each other as they walked down the street side by side. Inside the marshal's office, Sloane sat behind his desk and Turnbull flopped into an easy chair in one corner.

"I'm going to have to put you in a cell," the marshal observed quietly.

"The hell you are. I'm sitting out here until we square this thing with the judge."

"You can have a lawyer get you out or whatever," Sloane said. "It's all the same to me. But I'm taking you in on a murder charge, and that means you don't get to rest your ass on an easy chair in my office. Tom, I let you save face out there by not bringing you in at gunpoint. Don't make a mistake about one thing, though, I'm arresting you for murder and you're going behind bars."

A six-gun suddenly appeared in Turnbull's right hand. He got to his feet, keeping the marshal carefully covered.

Sloane shook his head and smiled. "Now what kind of fool notion have you in your head? What can you do? Bust out of here? Whether or not you shoot me, you'll be on the run. You came here of your own free will. Now you have to stay. Else you should have run out in the first place when you heard I was coming."

Turnbull nodded slowly and put his gun back in its holster. He unbuckled his gunbelt and placed it on the marshal's desk. "I don't like the idea of being in a cell."

"Who does?"

Turnbull placed a five-dollar gold piece on the desk. "Can you get me a bottle and a good meal?"

"I sure can." The marshal showed the mayor to his cell and locked the door behind him.

"I never thought I'd let you trick me into going behind bars," Turnbull said with a smile.

"I didn't trick you. I only did what any good marshal
does—gets people to stop being crazy and start being
sensible."

When the deputies came, he sent one for food and
drink for his prisoner, reminding all three men that the
mayor was innocent until proven guilty. Another hour
passed before they all heard a clatter of hooves outside
the office as the sheriff and some of his men arrived.
Cahoon came inside alone and nodded to the marshal,
who had taken the precaution of rising to his feet.

"I've come to take the prisoner into my custody," the
sheriff announced.

For all the marshal knew, the sheriff was entitled to
do this. Sloane wasn't given to studying law books. He
said, "You better find out what Judge Hayes thinks of
that."

"I'll take care of the judge in good time," Cahoon
barked. "First things first—you release Turnbull to
me."

Sloane took his time to think this over, more to give
Cahoon a chance to look at his own situation then to
figure out a move for himself. Sloane knew what he
would do. He would pull the same thing on the sheriff
as he had on the mayor. The only thing was that Cahoon
was not too bright, which might cause him to miss the
point.

"Seems to me Sheriff," the marshal drawled, "that
you're in a marshal's office with a courthouse just down
the street. If you and me have a custody problem, you
should solve it down there, not here. Sheriff, I'm asking
you to leave."

"I ain't moving without Turnbull," Cahoon grated.

Sloane saw he meant every word of this. "You come into my office, Sheriff, and make demands. What are you going to do if I don't go along with them? Shoot me? In order to break out a man charged with murder? That ain't a sensible act for any thinking man."

"That murder charge against Turnbull is just politics, put together by that durn judge and old Kringer. I'm gonna settle accounts with that judge. Now you let the mayor come with me."

Sloane went for his gun. He was still fast, although not as fast as he used to be. He'd taken to solving a lot of disputes of late through words instead of bullets, and this had caused him to lose his edge as a gunfighter. He didn't have it in him anymore.

Sloane saw this for himself as his gun cleared its holster and he thumbed the hammer back. He saw the killer blaze in Cahoon's eyes that Sloane's own victims had seen before they died. And he saw the Colt Peacemaker in Cahoon's hand, already cocked, its barrel raised faster and higher than his own. Knowing he had been outdrawn, Sloane made the instant decision to fire early, before his barrel was level, and hope to hit Cahoon in the leg and spoil his shot.

But it was Sloane's shot that was spoiled—by a .45 slug that stove in two ribs before shredding his heart. The marshal's bullet creased Cahoon's left thigh, burning through his leather chaps and leaving a bleeding furrow across his flesh.

None of the three deputies drew. Marshal Sloane lay dead on the floor. Mayor Turnbull walked out the door free.

Unknown to Earl Sloane when he entered the Star Saloon to arrest Tom Turnbull, Raider and Doc

Weatherbee were among those there and ready to lend him and his three deputies support, if they needed it. Doc had brought his Diamondback .38 revolver, one of the rare occasions on which he carried a weapon. When the mayor went quietly and none of his supporters tried anything, Raider and Doc kept in the background and did nothing. They had still not been uncovered as Pinkertons, and they hoped to keep it that way until the time came for them to act.

Staying on at the Star after the marshal and mayor had left, they knew that the sheriff was expected in town. Doc and Raider had no choice but to hang back and let things develop. Cole Brent had not yet spoken with them about his friend at the community, Henry Barlow. The two Pinkertons had only a vague idea who the farmers were that the mayor was accused of murdering. For the Pinkertons, this was a county matter, outside Baker City. Also, neither the judge nor the marshal were the kind of men who tolerated interference in their affairs. Cahoon and his men had arrived in town without notice and had gone to the marshal's office with no delay. Raider and Doc were still in the Star when word came that the marshal was dead and the mayor free.

"Nate said he was going to plug the judge next," one gunslinger boasted.

Doc and Raider slipped outside.

"Damn, I should have stuck with Sloane or stayed outside his office or something," Raider muttered when they were in the street.

"He would have ordered you away," Doc assured him. "Sloane would probably have figured you for the opposition."

"I know I could've done something to save him," Raider persisted.

Doc knew it was hopeless to argue with Raider while he was in this kind of mood. He said, "Let's see if we can save the judge. You go tell him who we are and that we want him to stay out on the Brent ranch until we can see the lay of the land."

"He won't go," Raider predicted.

Doc smiled. "That's why I'm sending you. I'll be outside his house in thirty minutes, ready to roll."

The judge lived in a two-story frame house on a short offshoot at one end of the main street. They had heard that the judge had gone there from the courthouse after hearing about the marshal's death. Raider was relieved to see no sign of Cahoon or his gunsels when he got to the house. He banged on the brass knocker. When he got no answer, he thought he might have arrived too late, that the judge was already dead or abducted.

Raider heaved against the door with his shoulder and felt it shudder in the doorframe.

"Hold off!" a voice bellowed from inside, instantly recognizable as that of the judge. "No great oaf like you is going to break down the side of my house. I have a .45 in my hand, and next time you push against my door, I'll be pushing bullets through from this side."

"Judge, this is Raider."

"I know who it is. I saw you coming from the window. Now I'd like to see you going."

"Judge, I'm a Pinkerton operative. So is the traveling physician, Weatherbee. You must have seen him around. He don't look too honest, but he's a genuine Pinkerton too."

Raider pushed his identification papers under the door and had to wait five minutes while the judge, in careful lawyer's fashion, read every word before he let him in. He explained to Judge Hayes, as quickly as he could, everything that had happened and how they had been hired by Daniel Brent.

"Grab some things," Raider told him. "We're moving you out to the Brent spread before Cahoon and Turnbull get a chance to murder you."

The judge waved his Smith & Wesson Schofield .45. "I'm staying put right here. You're going to have to murder me to make me move."

Raider let his face fall in great disappointment. "Hell, that's too bad, because we'd planned to use you. You were important in our plan. Well, I guess we'll find us someone else."

"What was I supposed to do?"

"Simple," Raider said. "Me and Weatherbee will catch them and you'll hang them."

"I'll come," Judge Hayes volunteered.

Weatherbee arrived shortly after with his wagon pulled by Judith. They persuaded the judge to lie down out of sight on a blanket among the boxes of medicine only after they had loaded on four kegs of fine whiskey from his house. He took no other belongings for his stay at the ranch.

Sure that no one had spotted the judge climbing aboard Doc's wagon, Raider stayed behind at the house. It was sundown, and Doc would make it to the ranch just after dark and stay the night there. Raider made himself comfortable with some old copies of the *Salt Lake Tribune* he found in the kitchen and a quart bottle of beer. Judging by the state of the place, the judge did his own housekeeping. Apart from a loaf of stale bread and two sprouted potatoes, there was nothing to eat. He finished with the newspapers when the daylight got so poor he could not read the print. He lit a lamp and placed it in the hallway where it could not be shot at through the windows but where its glow could be seen directly. He wanted them to think Judge Hayes was still in the house, so they wouldn't go looking for him elsewhere. Now that it was dark, they should be along soon.

Raider climbed the stairs and circulated through the four upstairs rooms, pausing to stare through each window into the darkness, looking for movement. When they came, they didn't even bother to sneak up on the house. There were about a dozen of them in the street, and, just as Raider had done, they rapped on the brass knocker. Then they shouted for the Judge to open the door to them, that they knew he was inside. Raider peered down from an upstairs window at them, trying to pick out Cahoon, Turnbull, or Fredericks among them, but he had no luck. They had sent their goons on this job. They must have paid them well, because no man, no matter how much of a wild dog he is, wants a judge's blood on his hands. It's too dangerous.

The men outside were yelling and hammering on the door, threatening the judge with what they'd do to him if he didn't let them in. Raider heard a pane of glass break at the back of the house and moved to the head of the stairs. He heard a window being raised and then running footsteps come through the house. Then a man stepped into the lamplight in the hall, making for the door to open it from inside.

"Up here," Raider called down to him before he reached the door.

The man spun around, his hand diving for his gun. The big Pinkerton drew his Remington .44 and the gun roared in the confines of the staircase. Aiming down at a forty-five-degree angle, Raider buried a .44 lump of lead high in the man's chest. It exited low in his back, tearing out a handful of flesh with it.

Raider came down the stairs fast and kicked the revolver out of the dying man's left hand. He was still on his knees and trying to explain something to the world before he left it.

Taking cover behind the wall, Raider used his left hand to lower the rear window the man had come through, and he set the catch again. He ran back upstairs and looked out again. The single shot from inside the house and no further sign of their comrade had quieted them down some. They now saw they weren't going to have it all their own way.

They were up to something, but Raider couldn't see what it was, since they kept to whatever cover they could find and the darkness hid most of their movements. What the darkness could not hide was flame. One of them held a twist of hay soaked in kerosene on the end of a stick while another put a match to it. He ran toward the house with the blazing hay.

Raider had to shoot through a pane of glass, which he knew would slow and possibly deflect the bullet, in order to prevent the house from being torched. He missed with his first bullet and scored with his second when the man was only six or seven paces from the house. The man fell on his back and the flaming hay landed on top of him. He screamed like a stuck pig as his clothes caught fire and the flames roasted his skin.

"Truce! Truce, Judge!" A man came forward, waving a white handkerchief. "Hold your fire and let us save him and we'll bother you no more tonight, Your Honor."

After they had quenched the victim and carried him

off moaning, spread-eagled between four of them, the others kept their word and left.

Raider waited some time before he slipped out the back window. He went along the rear of the houses until he came to the alley alongside Blind Danny's place. He thought of going for a drink in some saloon, but even he could smell the gunpowder on himself, which resulted from shooting indoors. He wouldn't take a chance on giving the game away, because the longer the mayor and sheriff believed the judge was in his house and capable of taking care of himself in a fight, the better it was for everyone out at the ranch.

Besides, he figured an early night once in a while couldn't do him any harm.

CHAPTER TEN

"To hell with the judge," Turnbull told Cahoon. "Leave him be. We can't go to one end of the town and attack him again in broad daylight after what went on last night. Everyone in town knows about it."

"Maybe we injured him," Cahoon suggested. "He didn't show at the courthouse this morning, and the court clerk was afraid to go to his house in case he would be shot."

"Forget him. None of the men got him, because he was the only one to fire any shots. They admitted that to us. We may be better off things turned out like this and he survived. Too much is going wrong for us in this town already. Even if I do stay here, though, I'm going to have to work something out in New Hammelburg— take care of those witnesses who say they saw me. Without their testimony, no charge against me will stand up in court."

"We should shoot them all."

"They'll be hard to find, Nate. You can be sure they won't be working by themselves out on the edge of some field where we can get at them. I reckon we've got to be more ambitious than that."

"What do you mean?" the sheriff asked.

"I ain't sure. More and more folks are saying my
Baker City days are numbered. They're afraid to say it
to my face, but I'm told by my informers they're saying
it behind my back. They say I've pushed everybody far
enough so that they're ready to fight me rather than be
pushed more. To tell the truth, I can see what they
mean. It's about time the worms turned."

Cahoon laughed. "That's only talk. While they're
still complaining loudly behind your back, you're safe
enough. It's when they get quiet that you have to
worry."

"Maybe," the mayor allowed. "All the same, that
murder warrant ain't just going to rise up and disappear.
So long as I have it over my head, I can't function in
this town as mayor."

The sheriff spat contemptuously on the boardwalk.
"Here we walk down Baker City's busiest part, and is
there anyone to say a word against us? Has anyone
dared call you a name? Or throw a curse after you?"

"Not that I've heard," the mayor said with irony.

"That's what I'm saying." Cahoon spoke as if rea-
soning with a child. "We got these bastards on the run.
They know it, even if you don't. All we need do is keep
them on the run. Think big. Plug that dumb judge. Ride
into the middle of New Hammelburg, knock Kringer on
his ass, and tell him we'll burn the place if he doesn't
sell us that downtown walnut grove right now. Bring the
papers along from the courthouse here, so everything is
ready and all he has to do is sign. Everyone will scream
fit to wake the dead. But I say let them. They all enjoy
the sound of their own voices."

Turnbull slapped Cahoon on the back. "Nate, you're
a tonic for a perpetual worrier like me. Sometimes the
answer is simple and direct. For want of any better so-

lution, I'm inclined to go along with what you say." He glanced across the street to the opposite boardwalk, where Daniel Brent was walking abreast of them. "By the way, there's one of the chief complainers and mischief makers in this town. After the judge, he's next to go."

The sheriff looked across at the blind man striding along as if he could see. Cahoon snickered. "Maybe he'll walk into something and kill himself. It shouldn't be hard to set up."

Raider was finishing breakfast at the hotel when Daniel Brent returned. He spoke first with his wife and then came across to Raider's table.

He sat next to Raider and said, "Some sons of bitches are so full of themselves they give no account to a man who learns to see with the skin of his face and to walk as fast as any other man. You'd think they might suspect he had developed very acute hearing, too."

Raider grunted concommittally, not knowing what this was all about and half expecting it to develop into some kind of attack on him. Raider admired Brent for his gutsy approach to life but didn't appreciate the way Brent had of wanting always to be boss man.

Brent detailed for the Pinkerton what he had heard from the far side of the street as Turnbull and Cahoon strolled along. "My wife and kids are getting ready right now to join Cole out on the ranch."

"You go with them," Raider told him.

"No way. I'm a city councilman and I'm sticking by my duty. Part of the trouble this town is in was brought on by me unknowingly. I aim to stand by and clear it up."

"There's nothing you can do."

"Sure there is," Brent said. "There's a meeting of the council today. The mayor might have something else interesting to say."

"It's your neck," Raider said. On getting back the previous night from the judge's house, he had told Brent what had happened and how Weatherbee had spirited the judge away to the ranch for his safety. "I reckon your wife and kids will be safe enough if they leave now. I'm going to head over to Jason Wymes's place and see if he can spare us some men who can handle a gun. Way things are going, we're going to need them real soon. Take care."

"Wait a moment, Raider. I've got something I want to ask you. Weatherbee will be out at the ranch. You think it's safe for my wife to be out there with him?"

"Hell, Weatherbee never could steal a woman off me," Raider lied. "All the same, I wouldn't delay too long in getting out there if I was you.

At the Wymes house in Baker City, Raider was told that the boss had left for the spread at first light. This was little more than an hour's ride outside town, so Raider saddled his mount at the stables and headed there. Even before he neared the ranch buildings, he saw the huge cloud of dust raised in the sky by the moving herd of cattle. A man standing by the corral said the boss was somewhere about.

Wymes was rushing around, getting the drive under way. When Raider asked him for men, Wymes laughed and said, "Ah, you thought you could put some of those I used for chasing Chinamen to better use? They're all moving out today with the herd. Look at them standing over there? What do they remind you of?"

Raider looked. "Like a ship's crew, the way you see

them being put together on the San Francisco docks."

"That hadn't occurred to me, but you're damn right. They sure don't look like no cowboy outfit. That one there was a soldier until recently, and the one next to him claims he's a preacher. Then there's two prospectors, a stage driver, a lumberman, and a dry-goods clerk. There's two more—the mean-looking ones next to the bunkhouse—and I don't want to know what they've done or where they've been. Two of these sons of bitches didn't even know how to ride a horse when I hired them a week ago." Wymes twisted his mouth into a sly grin. "By the time the drive is done, they'll be so used to horseback they'll have to learn again how to walk."

"What's to stop them deserting?" Raider wanted to know.

"For a man to be independent a few days out of town, he had to own his own horse and saddle, unless he's willing to pack his blankets on his back and walk. He'd have to be crazy or pretty damn mad to do that, and either way we'd be well rid of him. If he tried riding off, taking a mount with him, that'd be horse stealing. On the range, that's about worse than murder. He knows he'd be strung up for that. I have twenty-two beeves in this drive. The experienced hands are moving out the herd. Then when they're settled down, we'll put the "sailors" in charge of them. I supply everything except the men's bedding. For these nine men, and the trail boss, cook, and horse wrangler—twelve in all—I've laid on a wagon rigged for four horses, with hoops and a cover. It has a mess box in the tail, a water barrel on the side, and utensils, tin mugs and dishes, food supplies, and other stuff they might need. Each man gets his own saddle, bridle, saddle blanket, and forty feet of rope."

Raider accompanied Wymes as he took care of all kinds of last-minute arrangements. At the next lull in activities, he asked, "You think some of your regular hands might lend a hand after they're finished with the herd?"

"I'll help you myself when I finish here," Wymes volunteered, although Raider hadn't asked. "I live in town, so I know what bastards Turnbull and Cahoon are. But my men don't. They live out here and come into town to raise a little hell when they have some money. When they don't have money, they're not welcome and they know it. So what do they care about Baker City and who runs it? These are men who refuse to go on a cattle drive for me. I don't know what's going to make them want to fight for you. Anyway, why do you need them so bad right now?"

Raider decided he had to tell him. "We have information that Turnbull and Cahoon are making a move on New Hammelburg."

Wymes laughed. "Those bastards are getting crazier by the day. They must be eating locoweed along with their whiskey. No good you telling my men they should fight for New Hammelburg, though. You know how them Holy Joes out there have been denouncing saloons and soiled doves and poker games. If you tell my men Cahoon wants to get rid of them, it'll be like saying he's clearing the land of varmints. They'll more likely ride with him than you."

Raider laughed. He saw the truth of this. They went on to check the horses in the corrals. Although he knew he'd get little help here, Raider lingered on out of personal interest in the cattle drive. If he hadn't become a Pinkerton, he might be heading out on a drive like this himself. Ranch life appealed to him, and he wanted to see what he was missing by not having gone as a cow-puncher.

"Each man has eleven horses in his string," Jason Wymes was saying. "This is more generous than most drives allow, but I think it's an economy to have plenty of horses. Even when the going is easy, the animals are hard-worked, and they have to eat what they can find along the way, which often doesn't have much nourishment. Every one of these fat horses you see in these corrals is going to end the drive with his rib cage showing beneath his hide. One man may be harder on his horses than another. One man's string will be in good shape and another's will be all tore up, with the same amount of work."

"I'm a heavy man, and I'm hard on horses," Raider said.

"That's not really what I'm saying," Wymes went on. "A little skinny fella can cut his horse in pieces while a big man is gentle with them. It's not the weight alone that wears them down—though that's important —it's also the way a horse is handled. But what can I do? There's plenty of good horses here and a shortage of good riders. You'll see for yourself when it's time for them to ride out. They're awful. They've only tried out on gentle horses. I reckon they've to have some fun when they run up against ones still a bit green. They got a few outlaws here too."

Raider was aware that, to a rancher, any horse was "gentle" if he wasn't green, which meant unbroken and thus an unknown quantity, or an outlaw, which meant he was vicious, either through temperment or brutal handling while being broken. Raider had bit the dust a number of times from so-called gentle horses.

He was beginning to feel a little sorry for this motley crew who looked so ill prepared to take in excess of two thousand head of half-wild cattle across hills, rivers, and hundreds of miles of prairie to the railroad at Cheyenne. There were only a few points between the Blue Mountains of Oregon and the North Platte of Wyoming where a side of bacon or a sack of flour could be bought. Drovers often traveled two or three weeks without seeing a human being outside their own outfit. From Cheyenne, after the drive was over and they had been paid off, chances were most of them would not make it back to Oregon again, but maybe wander south to New Mexico or Texas—or in just about any direction where they thought life might be interesting. Of course some of them might have reason not to go in a particular direction, owing to a previous misunderstanding at some location out that way.

By now the herd was out of sight behind a rise in the land, though the column of dust raised by their almost nine thousand feet showed where they were. Wymes judged the herd was properly under way and that it was time for the horses and men to join it. Everyone mounted up to lend a hand, including Raider. There were fifty to sixty horses in each of two corrals, and all were to accompany the herd. The horses were skittish and excitedly running in a circle inside each corral. Instead of calming the animals down, Wymes, the trail boss, and the wrangler were shouting and cursing at the men and at each other, issuing what sounded to Raider like conflicting orders.

Raider didn't see exactly what happened, but one moment there was a corral full of horses and the next

instant it was empty. The horses bolted over the grassland, at first in a solid pack, then breaking into three
groups which traveled three different ways. The horses
still penned in the other corral got so excited they were
threatening to break the rails.

Wymes rode past Raider. His face was white with
rage. "Tell Cole Brent," he shouted to Raider, "that if he
wants to bring them Chinamen out here, I'll help them
kill as many of these bastards as they want and they can
ride in their place."

"I'm pleased to say that the *Sentinel-Advocate* has
settled down and completely recovered from being
seized by a lunatic who published the lamentable fig-
ments of his diseased imagination," Homer Fredericks
announced to the Baker City councilmen ranged along
the committee table with the mayor at its head. "The
printers and other workers were forced at gunpoint to do
the bidding of this maniac, and because of this I have
not dismissed them from their jobs. I know all of you
will be pleased to hear that the town's newspaper is
vigorous again and in responsible hands; however, it is
not for that reason alone I have brought up its existence
and prosperity at this meeting."

The councilmen sighed and their minds began to
wander. Homer Fredericks loved to talk—more accurately, to address meetings. The longer he spoke, the
more grandiloquent his words became. He usually kept
on until he lost track of what he was talking about, then
sat down abruptly.

"Today it is my sad duty to inform you that we have
a Judas among us," Fredericks announced in a dramatic
voice consciously modeled on that of Couldock in the
second act of *The Willow Copse*.

That caught everyone's attention. All eyes turned to him.

Homer Fredericks basked in their attention. "A monstrous traitor," he declaimed. "One who smiles in our faces and betrays us when our backs are turned. I will not look him in the eye for fear my emotions would overcome me before I could fully reveal his evil machinations to this council," Homer turned his face off to one side, so that his eyes would not be offended by the sight of the guilty one.

The councilmen looked at one another. This was not at all like Homer Fredericks. He usually rambled on about inconsequential matters. They all looked back at him.

Homer was not quite ready to deliver yet. "So that you will understand my accusation, I must provide you with some background, which I will keep brief. The replacement for my insane and now deceased employee had some recollection of a pair of names he came across in this town. He could not exactly recall where or when he had come across them before. With a true reporter's tenacity, he wrote to newspaper contacts elsewhere and an answer came by this morning's stagecoach. Raider and Doc Weatherbee are Pinkerton operatives." Fredericks paused for effect. "That might not be much in itself, gentlemen, were it not for why they are here. At first I believed Jason Wymes had hired them. But Wymes is not interested in this town. Also, he's not the sort to hire Pinkertons when he could have fast guns at a cheaper price. Then I saw I was missing what was right in front of my nose. Who are these Pinkertons staying with? Whose son went east for a short spell before they arrived? Maybe Daniel Brent will be kind enough to tell us why he brought them here."

Brent got to his feet, looking haggard and worn. Every man there respected him enough to wait until he had his say before they joined Fredericks in accusing him. All he said was, "Let me hear the sound of your voice once again, Fredericks."

"You certainly will hear it denouncing you," Fredericks thundered across the table.

Brent turned and faced his blind eyes toward him and said, "Thank you."

Then they all saw Brent whip out a .45 revolver and fire a single shot at the sound of the voice. The bullet entered Fredericks's mouth and broke away his spine from his skull.

Raider was ambling his horse down the middle of the street, trying to make his mind up whether to go to the Star or the Egyptian Palace and whether he should stable his horse or hitch him outside the saloon and ride on to the ranch. He had just ridden back from Wymes's spread with a promise from Jason to help out as best he could. Before Raider left town again, he wanted to check on Daniel Brent and, if possible, persuade him to go to the ranch. He also wanted to find out the whereabouts of Turnbull and Cahoon. He knew right away when he saw Blind Danny running out of the courthouse, firing wildly behind him with a revolver, that at least some of his decisions had been made for him.

The big Pinkerton spurred his horse, yelled to Brent, and pulled his carbine from its saddle scabbard, all in a matter of a couple of seconds. The carbine's short barrel made it ideal to use on horseback. He levered a shell in the chamber and hit the first man to show his face out of the courthouse in pursuit of Brent. The man went down in a writhing heap and kind of discouraged those following after him.

Having thrown three more bullets that shattered panes of glass in the courthouse windows, Raider switched his weapon and the reins to his left hand. He yelled again to give Brent orientation, though the sound of his horse's hooves were enough for that. Raider leaned down sideways to the right so that his arm crossed in front of Brent's body to catch the man's right upper arm from the inside, beneath the armpit. Instinctively Brent grabbed Raider's arm with his left hand and found his light body lifted off the ground and dumped on the horse's back behind Raider.

"Anyplace in particular you want to go?" Raider shouted over his shoulder to Brent as he cantered the horse out of town.

Shots and bullets whining past them through the air made it hard for them to talk.

CHAPTER ELEVEN

The ranch house was kind of crowded, with Daniel Brent, his wife and four children, including Cole, one of the two Pinkertons, six Chinese—one was still not well enough to move on, and the others were waiting for him—and Judge Hayes. Raider refused to go inside the house; he ate his food out by the corral and slept in the barn, since there was no bunkhouse.

Cole's friend from the Kringer settlement, Henry Barlow, had been to see him and asked that Doc and Raider come to New Hammelburg as soon as they could.

"I want to come with you when you go," Cole said to Raider when he brought his food out to him at the corral. "This place is getting on my nerves. That old judge is mean as a polecat and loco as they come. Now that my father has arrived and thinks everyone has to obey him because they're on his ranch, the sparks are flying. Doc just sits there, ignoring them and talking with my mother. Doc had better watch out or my father'll be gunning for him. He's already scowling at him and talking about sending him back to Chicago."

Raider laughed. "I ain't never one for crowd scenes. First thing tomorrow morning, Weatherbee and me is going to head out and see this preacher Kringer. I expect to meet up with Jason Wymes out there, if he ever got his horses rounded up and sent them beeves on their way. You come along if you're so inclined."

"See you in the morning, then," Cole said. "And, Raider, thanks for saving my father tonight. I owe you one."

"Then find me a beer for breakfast."

Not long after first light, Cole and Raider saddled three horses. They left one behind for Weatherbee, who would catch up with them. He was setting up the defenses of the ranch house for while they were gone. Doc caught up with them long before the cultivated fields of the settlement in the river valley came into view.

Once the three riders were spotted by the settlement farmers, there was a flurry of activity. Small groups of armed farmers rode every which way, some coming to meet them, others rushing off bringing warning of their arrival. Confusion was a polite word for what was going on.

"Cahoon and his men will cut through here like a knife through butter," Raider opined.

Henry Barlow was with the group that met them, and his friendliness with Cole eased the anxieties of the community members, who plainly did not take at all to Weat'erbee and Raider.

"I d you bring your straight razor, Doc?" Henry aske with a wink.

Weatherbee was mystified by this question and even ran his hand over his clean-shaven face to see if the youth was referring to some part he might very uncharacteristically have missed. Then he heard Cole hiss at Henry to shut up or Weatherbee would use his razor on him. Doc immediately guessed Cole had been spinning yarns, so he said to Henry in a smooth, menacing voice, "Making jokes about sharp objects can get a man's tongue cut out."

Henry stiffened and stayed well away from Weatherbee for the rest of the ride to New Hammelburg.

Jason Wymes was waiting for them in front of a three-story house with porches. All of the buildings here were better constructed and more elaborate than anything in Baker City, including the new courthouse. Wymes pointed out the walnut orchard that Cahoon and his comrades wanted to buy to open an "entertainment" section in the town.

"They figure that once they get a foot in," Wymes said, "they can make life impossible for the rest of the God-fearing folk and bit by bit take over the whole town. Judging from what you see, I know you'd say it was easy pickings. But these folk might surprise you. They're as tough and determined as anyone in Oregon, only they're not given to fighting. A group is gone to buy new rifles from a traveling dealer who's at some mines a few hours' ride from here. I figure you boys and me can shape up few fighting squads fairly quick. Raider saw how I put together a crew for my cattle drive. If I can make cowpunchers out of that lot, I'm dang sure I can make fighters out of these farmers." He laughed.

"How do we get started?" Weatherbee wanted to know.

"We have a few rituals to attend," Wymes answered. "Otherwise they won't be friendly to us. First we have to be presented to their leader, Dr. Kringer, and then we have to accept their hospitality by eating their food. They don't have hard liquor, but they make good beer. After that, but not before, we lay out plans to fight."

Dr. Kringer looked frail, yet there was no doubting

the intensity of his mind or the authority he held over the community members.

Kringer looked from one to the other of the four outsiders and smiled. "I know that we seem like strange folk in your eyes," he said in heavily accented but natural English, "but we do not really differ very much from you. As a community, we are one family. 'From every man according to his capacity, to every man according to his needs' is the rule that runs through our law of love. As between ourselves, we are many with one purpose. In contact with outsiders we are dealing with many, but with justice and honesty and neighborliness, withholding no solicitude or needed act of charity or mercy, and giving it without money and without price where there is any call for it, to the limit of our ability in money or food or clothing or service in sickness or in health."

They shook hands with him, he thanked them for coming, and they left.

They were brought to a large room in the middle of which was a revolving table. The circular table was more than eight feet in diameter, and attached to a support at its center was another smaller tabletop, about a foot higher than the one beneath it, which also revolved. All kinds of foods were piled on these tabletops, and a keg of beer, already tapped, lay on a nearby trestle.

It had been months since either Doc or Raider had seen loaves of golden bread and plates of butter, fresh fruits and vegtables, cinnamon-brown gingerbread cakes, fruit pies with rich juices staining the crisp crust, head cheese, fresh and salted meats, fish.

Raider downed a tankard of strong beer, wiped the foam from his mustache, and allowed as how there was something to be said for the farmer's way of life.

They ate meat pancakes, prospector's soup with sourdough biscuits, roast venison. The two Pinkertons left the smoked and salt salmon alone. They tried fern pie, made from the tender tips of young ferns, and liked it. They loaded up on huckleberry griddle cakes, apple turnovers called McGinties, blackberry pie.

Raider belched and said, "Takes your mind off fighting, sure enough."

These words had hardly come from his mouth when they heard a long series of scattered shots that seemed to be coming closer, plus some shouts and galloping hooves.

"It's Cahoon!" Raider yelled and made for the door, with the others right behind him.

They ran to their horses, leaped into the saddles, and rode out to meet the attackers. Farmers galloped their horses in every direction and loosed off shots from their long-barreled, old-fashioned rifles at imaginary enemies in clumps of trees.

"They're going to shoot more of each other than Cahoon will," Raider grumbled. He found what he was looking for—an area of high ground with some shade trees. "Spread out and stand still," he called to the others. "They have to pass us here to come into town. Take care to aim and bring down your man."

They didn't have long to wait. Retreating farmers were the first to pass. Then a horde of masked riders, firing as they came. At least thirty of them came in a massed bunch. The sight would have been enough to terrify a hardened Sioux warrior, let alone peaceful, food-loving farmers. Doc, Raider, Cole Brent, and Jason Wymes blazed away at them as they passed by. They brought down six riders.

When the masked men rode in among the clustered

buildings of town, suddenly gun barrels poked from
every window of every house. Men, women, and children used every weapon they had, even muzzle-loaders
and horse pistols. Most of them missed, but so many
people firing into a bunch of riders brought down some
men and horses. The shock they gave Cahoon and the
others was more effective than the actual damage they
caused.

Raider and the others rapidly reloaded their long
guns and rode up in the rear to provide support. When
Cahoon suddenly ordered a retreat, the Pinkertons and
their two comrades were caught in the open, directly in
front of the invading horsemen.

"Dismount!" Raider yelled and leaped out of his saddle. "Put your horses between them and you! Hold tight
on the reins!"

All four stood their ground, using their horses as
cover. Raider fired from beneath his horse's head, Doc
over his mount's back, using the saddle as a gun rest.
Wymes had a balky horse, which would not stay still.
Whether because it was still green or a bit of an outlaw,
it tore the reins from his grasp and bolted, leaving
Wymes standing there exposed. He tried to reach the
cover of Cole's horse but was cut down by two revolver
shots at close range by one of the passing horsemen.
Raider placed a bullet in the middle of the man's back
and tumbled him out of the saddle.

Jason Wymes lay on his back, one leg twisted beneath him, his eyes staring up at the sky and not seeing
the clouds.

They counted thirteen of Cahoon's men dead, among
them one city councilman.

"You can bet Cahoon and Turnbull were riding in

that pack," Doc said. "We did well enough, even if we didn't get either of them."

They carried the body of Jason Wymes indoors. Community members promised to build a coffin and ship the body to Baker City. Within the hour, women would leave to break the news to his wife and offer her their condolences.

"You expecting them riders back soon?" one farmer asked, nervously looking into the distance.

"I don't think they'll be back again today," Doc surmised. "I'm pretty sure they recognized us here. That means they'll probably pay a visit to the Brent ranch."

Cole became agitated. "My family is there. Come on, let's ride!"

It made him mad, the slow and easy way Doc and Raider were taking things, when they should have been riding hell for leather there.

"I say we should've stayed and gone in them buildings," Turnbull told Cahoon as they rode in front of their men, out of earshot as usual.

"Don't be stupid," Cahoon told him. "If I go into a house, a ten-year-old could shoot me dead, no trouble at all. There were dozens of houses, maybe hundreds of people. We'd have lost one man at least for every house we entered. I ain't been to school as long as you, but I did learn to add and subtract. That 'rithmetic would have been zero for us, any way you want to count it."

"We lost a third of our men," Turnbull complained.

"I know it."

"I don't think we should've run so soon. We could've waited a little longer before you gave the order."

Cahoon was used to men bitching under the pressure of combat, and he was coldly patient. "Tom, it takes a good commander to know when to turn tail. Your average idiot doesn't back off until he's lost most of his men. I saved most of yours by going when we did. Surprised them Pinkerton bastards, too."

"You sure we shouldn't have gone back for a second attack?" Turnbull nagged.

"For chrissake, Tom, these are hired guns we have here, not the U.S. Cavalry. They ain't going back in there to be shot like rats in a barrel no matter what we pay them. The only reason they're still riding with us after losing all their comrades is that I've promised them easy revenge at the Brent ranch, along with the women there and the cattle on the land."

"We could use some fun, Nate. Things ain't been going too well. How do you want to take the place?"

"You take half the boys and circle round the back, keeping out of sight. Then ride up quietly on their rear. When they spot you, they'll fire. That's when we'll charge full tilt from the front, while you come down at them from the back. It's open ground, but there's no way they can beat us off in a fast charge, 'specially not when the Pinkertons is at New Hammelburg."

Judge Hayes lay back in his easy chair, snoring loudly. Daniel Brent's wife, two daughters, and younger son were putting loaves of dough in the stove. The sick Chinese man was asleep on a pallet, three played a card game for matchsticks, and two kept watch at windows, one front, one back. Brent himself paced up and down, occasionally banging hard into things that had been moved to new positions. His uneasiness kept the others alert. Every so often he would poke one of the Chinese men on watch in the ribs to make sure he was paying attention.

This was the most relaxed the place had been for hours, due mainly to the fact that the judge was asleep and therefore not arguing with Brent.

The Chinese man at the back window said something, and the three playing cards jumped to their feet and talked rapidly in their own language.

"See who it is, Ben," Brent called to his younger son.

The youngster looked out the window and began counting out loud.

"What the hell are you doing, boy?" Brent shouted.

"Counting, Pa."

"What?"

". . . Eight, nine, ten. Ten horsemen, Pa. It ain't Cole and the others. These ones have bandannas over their faces."

Brent rushed to the window and pushed several of the Chinese away. "Gimme that gun. You handle the ammunition. Feed it in the gun, damn you. Ben, you are my eyes. Am I high? Am I low."

"Lower it, Pa. There. You got it now. Give 'em hell, Pa."

Brent blazed away with the Gatling gun Weatherbee had taken from the secret compartment beneath his wagon and mounted before he left. The multiple barrels revolved to avoid the overheating a single barrel would be subject to from rapid fire. As they revolved, the cluster of barrels one by one spat bullets as the blind man raked the approaching horsemen. One of the Chinese fed ammunition into the gun.

Two Chinese manned the Gatling that Doc had mounted in a front window. The sighted gunner needed only a few seconds of fire to scatter Cahoon's men when they attacked from the front, and those who couldn't escape died with their boots on.

The gunfight was all over before it had hardly begun.

"It just ain't natural using guns like these, Brent declared. "But there wasn't no other way to level them murdering bastards. Ben, son, give me your hand." He very seriously shook the small boy's hand. "I'm proud of you. You have courage and a quick mind."

"It must come from my side of the family, then," his wife said from the kitchen.

Just then Judge Hayes issued a loud snore from his easy chair, which was enough to cross the language barrier and make everyone laugh.

They saw the dead and dying, men and horses, on the open ground in front of the ranch house, and more behind it. Cole ran inside to see how his family had fared. The two Pinkertons, cold and professional, scanned the wounded and dead, sometimes pulling down a bandanna from a man's face. They knew some of them by name, others by sight. Cahoon and Turnbull were neither at the front nor the back.

"Only one place they could've gone," Doc said. "Baker City."

Raider nodded. "They ain't running out of the county just yet."

"Better leave Cole where he is and slip away."

Raider nodded again.

When they reached the town after an hour's ride, they had a difference of opinion on where to look.

Raider was naturally inclined to try the Star Saloon and
Doc the new courthouse. They solved their argument by
each going his own way.

Weatherbee knew he would find Tom Turnbull in the
records room of the courthouse. Everything the mayor
had done had involved deeds or paperwork shenanigans
of some kind. Now that he was in trouble, he would go
there to try to pull some other ace from his sleeve. Doc
only hoped Cahoon wasn't with him. For once he was
hoping Raider was right.

Doc heard Turnbull before he saw him. He was digging like a badger in the lowest drawer of a filing cabinet. Rustling the papers and pushing around the files, he
didn't hear the Pinkerton softly approach.

Taking a chance by not drawing his gun while he
could, Doc tiptoed behind the cabinet Turnbull was
rooting in. With a sudden lift and heave, Weatherbee
toppled the entire cabinet on top of him.

The cabinet wasn't heavy enough to cause him in-
jury, but it pinned him down long enough for Doc to
disarm him and snap manacles on his wrists.

"How come you didn't kill me when you had the
chance?" Turnbull asked.

"I'm leaving that to someone else," Doc said.

"Who? Raider?"

"No. Judge Hayes."

Cahoon was not at the Star.

"You seen the sheriff today?" Raider asked the barkeep.

The man shook his head and continued wiping the
countertop without a word.

Raider went along the street to the Egyptian Palace.
Cahoon was at the bar. He half turned as Raider came in

the door and called, "Give this man a glass of the best whiskey in the house. Pour me another. This time the winner pays."

The six or seven other customers along the bar took themselves off to far corners. Raider walked slowly to the bar, so that he was about a dozen paces away from Cahoon. The barkeep was so nervous he slopped some of Raider's drink as he put it before him.

"I want to drink a toast," Cahoon said. "Will you join me?"

"Depends on what it is."

Cahoon held up his glass in his left hand. "Here's to a new beginning or a bad end."

Raider held up his glass too, also in his left hand. "Winner pays," he said.

They watched each other raise the glass. The glass rims touched their lips at the same moment. They tipped up the glasses at the same time and tasted the smooth fiery liquor. Their right hands reached for their guns at the same moment.

The long-barrel .44 spat flame an instant before the Peacemaker .45. Nate Cahoon's body crumpled on the sawdust instead of the Pinkerton's.

Raider thought for a moment about how close a thing it was between him and Cahoon. Then he put it out of his mind.

JAKE LOGAN